TRAIL OF THE INNOCENTS
by
Al Cody

Author of "Squatter Sovereignty" *and*
"Badge of a Marshal"

Harley Keith had been successful in finding more
than his share of gold, in a country where it was
more dangerous to be rich than to be poor. Therefore he concealed his wealth from the cutthroats
who would gladly have killed him for it and set out
to meet his friend Jim Burden. He came across Jim
—hanging from a gallows tree—and knew that his
own trials had only begun. For Burden had been
murdered by a band of outlaws who signed themselves: 3-7-77, who were ironically known as The
Innocents and who had long-range plans which they
were bound and determined to bring to eventual
fruition.

And Keith now stood in their way!

TRAIL OF THE INNOCENTS

TRAIL OF THE INNOCENTS

by

AL CODY

MAGNUM BOOKS
NEW YORK

PLAYMORE, INC., PUBLISHERS
and WALDMAN PUBLISHING CORP.
New York, New York

Printed in the United States of America

TRAIL OF THE INNOCENTS

1.

Inside the saloon misnamed The Golden Promise, the air hung heavy and torpid, fogged with stale cigar smoke and the accumulated odors of a low-ceilinged room habitually crowded and poorly ventilated. Outdoors, humid air blanketed the valley, hanging oppressively against the hills, the heat of afternoon squeezing down until the ground seemed to sweat. Thunder rumbled in the jumble of hills to the west, heavy as ore wagons crossing a bridge. Clouds which belonged to midnight, shot through with sulphurous crimson, were piling along the rim of the gulch, blotting out the banked fires of sunset.

The game at the faro table came to a temporary pause as the no longer affluent tenderfoot pushed back, then walked glassily out into the open, his breath shallow with shock. Keith watched him go with brief compassion. At least the man hadn't made the mistake of trying to buck his opponents with a gun. He who lived could learn.

Rarely, during any twenty-four period, did the game cease entirely. Players came and went in endless procession, miners flushed with luck, pokes bulging; lean, rangy outriders with watchful eyes, dangerous men of careful courtesy; the restless element who never worked but were always affluent, the scourge of that raw land; strangers and tenderfeet. The dealers gave no sign beyond a brightening of the eyes or a tightening of the jaws. They worked in monotonous, cigar-chewing shifts, supple fingers never far from the cocked revolvers beneath the rim of the table.

A bartender mopped briefly at spilled liquor, raw whiskey on which the tenderfoot had choked. Harley Keith, after a glance through the open door, climbed wearily down from the lookout's stool, limping slightly as he set his weight squarely upon his feet. This would be his final session in The Golden Promise and in the town, but he would leave with as little regret as any of the occupants were showing at his departure.

Only once in half a year had he seen a genuine show of grief for anyone. Lou of the yellow hair had wept unashamedly as the life bubbled redly from the twin bullet holes in Ole Arvard's lung. Ole had been a giant of a man, as kindly as he was strong, and there had been a light in Lou's eyes when she looked at him. They never brightened now, though the grass grew green above his grave.

Keith's long, lean frame appeared to descend in sections from the high stool, and the unruly shock of yellow hair lay over his left eye, as it usually did. Not that the masking lock caused any handicap. Players had been heard to observe that Keith could see more with one eye than most men managed with two.

He glanced briefly toward Lou, but she was gazing out a far window. Friedlund, owner of the faro layout, had his money ready. Keith had informed the gambler earlier in the week that this would be his last shift, that he was moving on. Friedlund came from a back room, silent as the summer wind, draped as always in funereal black from neck to boots, unlighted black cigar half-shredded between powerful teeth. His single concession to the heat had been to unbutton the fancy black velvet vest.

His high pointed chin moved in a barely perceptible nod, and he shoved a small sack of dust and nuggets across the table, his gaze already carefully appraising as a new player slid into the vacated chair. This man's breath reeked of whiskey, but not strongly enough to overcome the strongly unwashed odors of body and clothes. Friedlund's thin nostrils became pinched, and his gray eyes grew stonily remote. Otherwise he gave no sign.

Keith accepted the pouch with an equal display of casualness, thankfully filling his lungs with fresh ozone as he stepped outside. The job as lookout had provided eating money while his left foot healed from an injury suffered in a mine shaft. It had also furnished a reasonable cover for his existence in the town, giving the lie to any possible suggestion that he might possess wealth beyond what was needed for the bare necessities of the day.

Neither the faro table nor the mine had held any particular appeal for him, and now he would be logically free of both. That was to the good, since he had no wish to spend the coming winter there, in that long, snake-like series of loosely connected mining camps. Towns snakelike in more ways than one, he reflected grimly—made up of men ever ready to strike in sudden, unreasoning fear and savagery, holding other men's lives cheaper than the dust for which they toiled.

Somewhere, as he stepped outside, a gun mocked the receding thunder. A bearded pack-rat of a man paused and raised his head in a listening attitude, but others along the street ignored the sound. They kept on with whatever they were doing, with complete indifference.

The thunder was late and out of time, but guns were always in season along the winding, endless gulch. Rarely did a day pass without at least one man dying of a neighbor's rancor, somewhere between the mouth of the junction and the wind-swept heights of Summit.

Between those points, towns had grown as carelessly as weeds and with as little planning, becoming crowded like peas in an overripe pod. Adobetown. Nevada. Central City. Virginia City. Pine Grove. Highland. Together they occupied a valley of gold and guns, bright with hope, dark with despair.

Keith had seen plenty of both during his stay: men and women who came and went, often making a sudden exit via Boot Hill, where dreams were done. It had been Washington Territory when he'd arrived, and it was Idaho now, and those who counted as old-timers in a land where life flowed as swiftly and trickily as quicksilver could remember when it had been Oregon Country. Gold had made the difference, hastening change, quickening man's ambitions to offset the enervating effect of summer heat or winter cold.

Seldom in the annals of prospecting had so rich a strike been made as in this gulch among the hills known as the Tobacco Roots. Even the glamour of Bannack had paled, if not the greed.

Far to the east, men waged grim warfare for the preservation or the tearing apart of the Union; to free enslaved men or maintain an order as ancient and as savage as man. But here, men dug for gold and then quarreled or killed for possession of the spoils, carelessly shrugging aside their country's travail. Here it was each man for himself, with the devil laughing from the brush.

It made for an exciting existence, and always a watchful one for those who would survive. Keith had found a certain pleasure in accomplishment, but he would have few regrets at leaving the country behind.

If all went well, this would be not only his last night in Pine Grove, but his last anywhere along the golden gulch.

He was conscious both of a mild pride in his accomplishments during the year, and of a cynical contempt for his achievements. The latter stemmed from his manner of befooling others into the apparently accept belief that for all these months he had barely managed to exist.

Which befits a coward turned brave only because of the circumstances, he mocked himself, then set off as briskly as his still sore foot would permit toward his own cabin. It squatted, aloof from most of the others, at the edge of the gulch. A towering boulder, which gave the illusion of being balanced precariously above, overshadowed it.

Illusion or not, the hundred tons of stone had hung unmoving for centuries longer than the white man had known the land. Keith had discerned the possibilities of his fortress-like neighbor, which was one reason he was already counted as one of the old-timers along the gulch. He merged in its deeper shadow, sidling away from his own door to a notch-like opening where he could stand sheltered and unobserved. The lookout afforded a perfect view not alone of his door but also of the single window of the cabin.

Twice during the summer he had detected uninvited guests and prepared accordingly. This time there was no sign of any disturbance, and he let himself in as a few drops of rain spattered warningly.

The chance of the shack's location was due to no plan of his. He'd bought the cabin when the gulch was greening after a long winter, the second day following his arrival in the town. He'd paid the owner a hundred dollars for the dwelling, with title to a claim thrown in. Either way, it had seemed a dubious transaction. The sodded roof was adrip whenever it rained; the claim had already proved worthless. Guffawing neighbors had shaken their heads at the luck of the owner making such a sale, while enjoying a tenderfoot's discomfiture.

Keith had not been unduly perturbed, having required only a shelter, a place to pause awhile, in his endless trek to nowhere.

More from curiosity than out of hope, he'd tried his hand at mining, working his claim, concealing both his surprise and elation when on the very next day he'd sunk his pick into gravel peppered with nuggets. The corner spot had seemed so unlikely that no one had bothered with it before.

He had already seen and heard enough to realize that riches could be a swift ticket to the plot known as Boot Hill, located on a cheerless, wind-swept knob beyond the town. Tales of murder were legion, with new accounts added every day. They ranged from the robbery of Bummer Dan to the killing of Lloyd Macruder.

It was comparatively easy to make money along the gulch; nature had distributed gold with a prodigal lavishness, often hiding it no deeper than at grass-roots level. To live long enough to enjoy new wealth was the trick.

Keith had watched giant, bearded Bill Fairweather roar up and down the gulch, scattering gold to a scrambling horde with wild abandon. For his own part, he'd played it cannily. He'd toiled alone, admitting that he was taking out gold, but only to the extent of wages on which a man could eat. The gold which he dug he hid, planning carefully how it might be gotten out of the country, beyond the reach of the road agents who brazenly called themselves The Innocents. Finally he'd hit upon a scheme which seemed to have merit.

The plan involved abandoning work on his own claim and turning instead to blacksmithing, in which he had a fair amount of skill. Since the strike had turned out to be no more than a pocket, which he'd already emptied, his disgust with the claim lent credence to the notion that it had been no better than his neighbors had prophesied.

In his spare time, when able to work unobserved, Keith had hollowed out the heavy bolster of a wagon, later packing the opening full of dust and nuggets. Still not confiding his secret to anyone, he was sending out a cargo of freight. The driver would probably prove trustworthy, having no inkling that he was seated above a fortune.

Keith had maintained the pattern of restlessness, of a man hounded by failure, giving up the smithing to toil in another mine, then, following his injury, acting as lookout for the faro game at The Golden Promise. Now, clearly broke and disillusioned, he was pulling out ahead of the coming winter.

The course he was taking might well mean leaving greater riches still in the ground, but he preferred that gamble to being known as affluent, and thus surely marked for death. Once the freight was delivered to Fort Benton at the head of navigation, he'd take over his own wagon, then turn the gold over to Well-Fargo.

It would be a good trick if he could work it. Keith was far from sure if his luck would run that far. Yet a man could do no less than try. He squinted at the clouds, then set about cooking a meal. There was an increasing feel of rain in the air.

There was only one thing to delay his departure, one possible hindrance to his private plans. That was the meeting of the Vigilantes which had been called for that night. Keith had a feeling that it might prove grim.

He could pass it up if he chose, getting a horse, then riding fast and far, clear out of the country. Other men had done the same thing more than once—at least many had tried, though there was no certain tally as to how many had succeeded. Some bodies had been found; other men were known to have disappeared, under circumstances which would not bear too close inquiry.

Self-preservation was as ancient as man; weighed against that were the friendships he had made during the hot summer and long autumn, the councils he had been invited to attend, and the obligations arising out of those conferences. Men such as Biedler, Sam Langford and Don Byam had done him the honor of trusting him. You couldn't ride out on such men.

Put simply, he had taken his oath as one of the handful of men opposed to the terrifying power of The Innocents and sworn to bring them to book, to restore order in a lawless land.

A splatter of rain lashed the scraped deerskin window as he finished his supper. Outside, the gulch was a pocket of gloom, squeezed so tightly that it leaked. Keith blew out his candle, and the reek of tallow mingled with the smells of boiled bear meat and cabbage. A wind swept from the head of the gulch, adding to the sudden rawness of fall, whipping against his face.

Keith stood a moment, stooping as much from habit as from necessity, a tall man inherently distrustful of average doorways and passages. He shook the rebellious lock of hair away from his left eye, setting his hat solidly. Rain had freshened the air, and he breathed deeply, filling his lungs.

A few lights shone yellow through the rainy night.

The clouds revealed a ragged tear, where a star gleamed like a polished nugget, and the moon strove to shove into view. Showers seldom lasted long.

He hesitated, not liking what lay ahead, but committed. Duty was a binding word, but it could be obnoxious.

Well, someone has to do the job, he reminded himself. The country has to be cleaned up—no doubt about that. Then he voiced his real dislike of the involvement. But in the process, and in view of some of the methods we have to use—are we much better than murderers ourselves?

That question had bothered him increasingly of late. But mulling over the right or the wrongness of his position served no good end. There were plenty of possible answers, and a man could accept or discard them, according to his own conscience.

That was the crux of it. Tonight, here in Alder Gulch, a man had to die. His doom had already been decreed, and the realization was strong in Keith that his guilt or innocence would have little to do with how a man felt when he choked in a noose.

On the other hand, it was proven guilt which was bringing the man to so distasteful an end, and he would deserve his punishment for what he'd done, wantonly and deliberately. Keith set out, taking a short cut among the weeping trees. A distant light, like a low-hung star, was a guide if he needed it, which he did not. He possessed a cat's instinct for the darkness, an ability to head unerringly toward a goal.

A light burned in the house of Fat Jake O'Hoon. Not much could be said about Jake except that he was always courteous. This might be a cover for less pleasant attitudes, but in the absence of proof, no one was bothering him. The meeting was to take place in the still darkened cabin, two doors beyond O'Hoon's.

"Sure and it's a fitting night for such meetings and such deeds," Keith grunted under his breath. "Murder, sudden death and damnation—they go together!"

The wind brought a last slap of rain, and with it a creeking sigh, like a failing breath. The moon rode suddenly in a serene field of blue, and Keith halted with a gasp, choking his outcry to a gurgle. The moonlight washed his face with a matching silver.

He stared, unbelieving, at the object which swung gently in the wind. Even in that gulch, which had often known sudden death, this was hard to credit.

At the same time it was dreadfully real. He had all but blundered against a man who hung suspended by a rope about his neck. Like the trunk of a tree, the rope divided into roots, forming a noose. Higher up, the single trunk was lost among the gloom of the real branches overhead.

2.

The Indians had had their own names for the trio of rivers, names which the white men, with unthinking arrogance, had scarcely even bothered to learn. For half a century now they had been known as the Madison, the Gallatin and the Jefferson, before they made a juncture to form the Missouri. This meeting place was appropriately called Three Forks, and at it a stopping place, a dubious lodging for the night, had been erected beside the road.

This halfway house could be called homelike only by a violent effort of the imagination. It was a log building, long and low, squatting with its back to the newly formed, somewhat sullen Missouri. On one side, cottonwoods strove to hide it, abetted by willows on the other side. The road in front was dusty and lonely.

Despite the existence of the road, horsemen along it were not too common, especially those who wore skirts. This particular skirt, forced up by the necessities of the saddle, revealed a pair of trim ankles and unusually pretty knees.

The possessor of the knees pulled to a halt, surveying the house frowningly, somewhat relieved at reaching it, yet disliking its looks and its reputation. She held her nervous horse steady as someone lurched around the corner by the cottonwoods, then staggered toward the doorway.

For a moment the girl's displeasure was reflected in her gray eyes, beneath frowning brows. The woman making so uncertain a passage was gray-haired, slovenly, and apparently drunk. Then, with a smothered cry, the girl was off her horse and running to aid the woman as it became apparent that the trouble was not due to liquor but to illness or injury. She caught the older woman as she reeled and almost fell. Using all her strength, she got the door open and helped her through.

The sick woman opened half-closed eyes, surveying in astonishment the stranger who had come to her assistance. Inside, she braced herself, one hand against the door jamb.

"Lord love us! There's still miracles."

Breathing raggedly, she jerked her head in a gesture toward an open door.

"My bed, dearie—in there."

Actually it was no more than a crude bunk, unmade, looking as uninviting as the remainder of the place, but the girl eased the sick woman onto the blankets.

She subsided with a sigh, eyes closed, face bloodless, and with a gasp she seemed to quit breathing.

Close to panic, the girl made a survey of the larger public room. Bottles and glasses were ranged on a shelf along one end, and a long table, its smoothed log top bare of any covering, filled half the room. Flies clustered on sticky, half-emptied tin plates, or buzzed restlessly about the room. A heating stove, surprisingly well blacked, made up the only other article of furniture, aside from chairs.

Uncertain yet determined, the girl took down a brown bottle. Though it was unlabeled, she had no trouble guessing at its contents. Drawing the cork, she poured some of the liquor into a tin cup. This she placed at the woman's lips, holding her partly erect with her other hand, forcing a swallow or so into her mouth.

The effect was as stimulating as she had hoped. The older woman gasped, choked, and her eyes opened again. She gazed at the girl a moment with tired but incredulous eyes, then obediently drank the rest and lay back with a sigh.

"Thanks," she gasped. "I sure needed that. I don't think I could have made it by myself. Where'd you come from, dearie?"

"I was on my way—and saw you." It was scarcely an adequate explanation, but it would have to suffice. The eyes in the haggard face grew keener.

"You mean—Good Lord, girl, you ain't alone?"

"Yes."

"That's bad, dearie—bad, in this country." Again the eyes focused appraisingly on the younger face, meeting the half-uncertain, shy stare of gray eyes, noting the smoothness of cheeks which blossomed with an added stain of color at the scrutiny. It was an oval face, beneath a soft pile of hair which matched the browning leaves outside. "You're a good girl," she pronounced, almost as though disappointed at the verdict.

"I—yes, of course."

"Which makes it worse—in some ways. Good Lord —and me this way—as if I hadn't problems enough—"

"You should rest," the girl protested. "You're not well. Never mind about me—"

"Better to mind about you while I have the chance." Faint asperity crept into the tone. *"I* don't count—I've had my day, such as it was. But you—alone. Don't you know that this ain't no country for women—special if they're young and pretty and decent?"

The gray eyes widened at the older woman's earnestness, her evident concern.

"I'm pretty good at looking after myself," she asserted, but her straying glance belied her bravery, revealing her apprehension. "Anyhow, I thought that Western men were chivalrous—"

The old head nodded slightly, as though her worst suspicions had been confirmed.

"You're a tenderfoot, dearie, like I guessed; a lamb among wolves. Chivalry—" Her laugh was short, harshly broken. "The Innocents stop at nothing—oh, Lordy!"

The girl was swiftly contrite. "You *are* sick—and you're bothering about me. What can I do?"

"I wish I knew. Sure I'm sick—this time I reckon I'm ready to cash in. The pain took me sudden and mighty sharp, out by the barn. I'd guess it's my heeart—except that nobody'd believe that Old Meg had such a thing."

"I don't think that you should talk so much."

"Now's the time to talk, while I can." The craggy face softened, and the harsh voice grew almost gentle. "It won't make any difference to me, dearie, and if it does—who cares? But you're young and good—and you've tried to help, to be kind to me. It's a long while since anyone's been kind to Old Meg," she added.

"You poor soul!" the girl said gently, and her soft palm rested against the troubled forehead. "You've had it hard."

"Sure I have. Who wouldn't, in this country?" Worry was manifest in her eyes. "Lordy, I'd give a lot to have a few more days—hours, even, to stick around and look after you. Only I ain't going to have no more time." She gasped, pain blanching her face, then went on, her voice barely above a whisper.

"It's too late to help the dying—but not the living. Listen, dearie, and do what I say. Maybe it'll help some—if you play your part right. That counts for a mighty lot. I've got a wig—in that bureau. Made of my own hair—I was scared I'd go bald. Think of Old Meg being that vain! But I was pretty once—near as pretty as you, though no one'd believe that now."

She recalled her straying thoughts with an effort.

"You put it on—dress up and fix up like me. Pretend you're Meg—you've got to. Act tough and mean, like I do—keep men scared of you and halfway respectful. Bend closer, while I tell you."

Obediently, frightened, the girl obeyed. She was wide-eyed but calm when she straightened, gently closing the lids above eyes which now looked on some new scene, far removed.

3

Shivering and appalled, Keith looked closer. The lynched man's head lolled at a grotesque angle, while the rope creaked protestingly as the body swung to the stir of wind. The face, almost on a level with his own, was terribly familiar.

Here was a warning, revenge, and reciprocal terror engendered by the men who signed their handiwork with the symbol 3-7-77. The Innocents had retaliated with treatment in kind.

The man in the noose was Keith's friend, Jim Burden. Keith had been expecting to meet him at the conference called for that evening.

Dark stains blotched Burden's shirt front. A closer look showed the reason. The hanging was sufficiently grim in itself, but the rope had not been the cause of death. Burden's throat had been cut before he was elevated—a wide, deep slash, which ran almost from ear to ear.

Fighting an inclination to sickness, Keith looked

about. The ground, hard-packed and barely moistened by the shower, revealed no clues. After a moment he went on. There was nothing that he could do for Burden, nothing that anyone could do. But the others had to be told.

He skirted Fat Jake's cabin, seeing the shadowy outline of a man inside through the dirty window. Fat Jake's was one of the few cabins in Pine Grove which boasted a glass window. An odor not unlike that of boiled onions emanated from it, staining the breeze. Boiled leeks, in all likelihood, since they grew close at hand. Fat Jake was something of a culinary artist.

The door to the second cabin was closed, and no light was showing. Keith rapped softly, a coded knock. The door swung silently inward, and a face, a blotch of white against the gloom, stared at him. Lips formed his name.

"Keith?"

"Yes."

"Then come on in."

When the door closed behind him, the darkness seemed total. Keith became aware of the repressed breathing of other men, still felt the clamminess which had gripped him beneath the tree. A voice spoke softly.

"We're waiting for three more. As soon as Law, Burden and McManus get here, we'll go ahead."

"Burden won't be coming," Keith said. His voice sounded strange in his own ears. "He's dead."

Sounds, to senses alert to them, could be almost as revealing as sight. He heard a gasp, a shocked cry of protest and disbelief from the opposite side of the room.

"Dead? What're you tellin' us?" The voice belonged to Landstrum. His long full beard, faintly touched with gray, was invisible, yet his voice maintained the impression of a patriarch. "He can't be! Why, I was talking with him not an hour ago—"

"I wouldn't doubt that," Keith agreed. "But a man can die fast. They've got him. I found him hanging, on my way here. Come along and I'll show you."

He sensed their hesitation, the oppressive sense of trouble. After a muttered word or so, they agreed and followed. The moonlight was stronger now, the clouds drawing away as though anxious to disperse after the discovery they had made. Keith indicated the body in silence.

The others walked around, saying nothing while they studied the available evidence, forming their own conclusions. Again it was Landstrum who broke the silence.

"Let's get him down," he said tightly. "Someone climb. I'll get some slack in the rope."

Keith climbed. Disregarding the blood, Landstrum clased the body to his chest and lifted, and presently they lowered Burden and carried him to the cabin. This time, a lamp was lit, smelling evilly of coal oil.

They faced each other in the light, rage and grief and a shadow of mistrust on many faces.

DuPree asked the question that was on every tongue. An old knife scar on his right cheek was livid.

"Just what do you know about this, Keith?"

"Nothing more than what I've told you. I took the short cut from my cabin—and found him. Then I came on to report."

"This is bad business." Landstrum's voice was heavy. "Did anybody see anything—any time?"

"It looks to me like a case of treachery—a double-cross," DuPree pronounced angrily. "Where are Law and McManus?"

"I was wondering about them," Landstrum admitted. "Well?"

"Who else would know about the meeting or have any reason for killing Burden —in such a fashion?" DuPree went on, and his logic sounded grimly reasonable. "There's always been something between those three—distrust; maybe worse."

"They had all taken the oath."

"One who will rob and kill will lie, too. Also, there is something which may have a connection. Just before it grew dark, I saw someone running near the far end of the street. In the rain and dusk, I couldn't be sure, and at the time I thought little about it. But it looked like Law."

"Law?" Mulvaney ejaculated. An excitable man, the

word popped from him like the crash of a small-caliber pistol. "At the end of the street? The stage must have been about to pull out."

"I didn't notice, but it's likely."

"The stage for Benton," Landstrum amplified carefully. There was a heavy silence as they considered the implications of this. "It seems to add up to treachery in our own ranks. I had hoped it might never happen —though lately I've had fears and doubts. In any case, treachery is the one thing we can't tolerate. If anyone— or more than one—gets away with this, we'll never succeed in cleaning up the country."

Under his challenging gaze, the others nodded sober agreement. Lawlessness, exemplified by brutality and a callous disregard for human rights, had been too long rampant. When the situation had grown intolerable, they had set out to do something. Some strong blows had recently been struck for law and order.

What had been accomplished was only a beginning. Now, if their own ranks had been infiltrated, if they were to be mocked in such a fashion—

"Our society must be inviolate," Landstrum added heavily. "Treason must be punished swiftly and surely. Otherwise The Innocents will be party to our secrets, to the names of all of us, privy to all our plans. No man's life will be safe, and justice in the land will become more than ever an empty slogan and a mockery. That we dare not permit."

"What you say is true; and for self-preservation alone, not to mention other reasons, the guilty must be hunted down," Mulvaney concurred grimly. "That is imperative. Jim Burden was a good man," he went on somberly. "And he has a wife somewhere in the East."

"We must catch up with Law," Landstrum pronounced. "Also McManus, unless he turns up and can explain himself. We must be sure before we act— suspicion is not enough. But once we are certain, justice must be meted out, inexorably, pitilessly."

"I dont think we'll have any reason to feel pity," DuPree growled.

"Conditions being as they are, we can spare only a single man for this pursuit," Landstrum went on. "I am assuming, in the absence of both suspects, that one or both is actually in flight. When the man who is picked overtakes the fugitive or fugitives, it will be up to him to discover the truth, to be certain. That may be difficult, but it must be done. Then, once he knows for sure—it will be his duty to serve as executioner."

No one contradicted him. However grim, it was justice.

"The pursuit, once undertaken, must be continued, no matter how far it goes or how long it takes."

Eyes strayed to the stiff, motionless figure, now lying on a blanket on the floor at one side. There was a stern nodding of heads.

"The fairest way will be to draw lots," Landstrum

went on. "It will probably entail a sacrifice for whoever is chosen, but we have agreed to do what must be done, regardless of the cost. Certainly this task will not be easy or pleasant."

Shrugging, he stooped, coming up with a thin stick of firewood. It made small popping sounds as he broke it into varying lengths. Then he lifted a hat from its peg against the wall and dropped the pieces in.

"We'll all help check to make sure that the others have really left town," he added. "After that—short stick does it. Reach across and draw."

The hat was placed on a box, below the rim of the table, where no one could see. They drew in turn, holding up their sticks to view. Keith, feeling his own, was conscious of a tightening of his stomach, though not from surprise. Somehow he'd anticipated nothing less.

"Looks like it's up to you, Keith." Landstrum nodded gravely. "Good luck—and watch your step!"

4.

Fate has a way of giving ironic twists to circumstances. Because he himself had suffered as a result of his name, Law's father had carefully named him Sebastian, choosing an unlikely moniker, determined that his son should not be handicapped by an unwelcome nickname. Perhaps it was precisely because Sebastian was both unusual and difficult, or because one particular name fitted with Law as naturally as a glove to a finger, what his father had feared had come to pass, and Sebastian, who was no lawman, was known as John Law.

The darkness was box-like, which was hardly to be wondered at, since it was night and he was virtually encased in a box. Resignedly and somewhat painfully, Law twisted about, elevating his knees, rolling head and shoulders, seeking a more restful position where none was to be found.

The last lurch of the speeding stagecoach had tossed him into a corner, his neck doubled and corded, head butting ineffectually against the triple corner formed by the floor and sides of the coach. Some earlier passenger had dropped a cigar butt carelessly on the floor, and its stale odor seemed to grind into his nostrils, even as the brittle leaves of tobacco ground into his face.

Momentarily his position eased; then another wild lurch of the plunging vehicle tossed him back and down, as painfully doubled up as before. This road through the Tobacco Roots hills was poor, even by stagecoach standards. Deep, twisting ruts, cut by the wheels of freight wagons, had made it worse than usual. Nor did the driver on the box appear to have any feeling of consideration for his lone passenger.

Law twisted again, and by a supreme effort heaved to a sitting position, shoulders against the seat, and legs braced against the opposite corner. He felt the warm trickle of blood from a cut on his neck, as it dribbled into a corner of his mouth. The thongs which tied wrists and ankles were drawn painfully tight.

He shook his head, partly to clear it of a sense of fuzziness, partly in resignation. About now, his fellow Vigilantes should be meeting at the old cabin near Fat Jake's, and they'd be wondering what had become of him. They might entertain suspicions concerning his loyalty to the cause when he failed to show up.

There wasn't much he could do about that. He hadn't seen the pair who had jumped him, striking from the gathering gloom without warning. One, he knew, had wielded a club, which, slanting down across his skull and the side of his head, had almost driven him into oblivion. The side of his face where it had raked was swollen and almost as sore as a boil.

A second man had caught him as he fell and dragged him back, away from the path, among tall bushes. There they had trussed him like a fowl for the roasting, then, as the stagecoach pulled up briefly in an unscheduled stop, had slung him inside and closed the door. The coach had taken off again with no noticeable delay.

His head was clearing sufficiently so that he could think again, assessing his position realistically if wryly. He'd tried shouting, without much hope, and had given up when it became apparent that the driver had closed his ears to all sounds of distress.

It was not surprising that the driver might be allied with The Innocents, since the outlaws were not only a widely scattered but also a tightly knit organization. Only that afternoon, Law had stumbled upon an astounding piece of news. It had seemed so surprising at first as to leave him flabbergasted, but after mulling it over, he had decided that it was not so very surprising after all. It bolstered other information which he'd planned to convey to the others at the evening meeting.

It might well be that what was happening to him was due to what he'd learned, was aimed at preventing his passing it on. Naturally The Innocents, particularly the man in question, did not want it known that their chief was also the head man of the law, none less than Sheriff Henry Plummer.

The surprising factor was that he was still alive and taking such a ride, instead of being killed outright. However, on second thought, there might be sound reasons. Others might be waiting somewhere along the line to ask questions—prying ones which, should he decline to answer, could make the present unpleasantness seem like comfort personified.

There seemed no doubt but that the road agents were becoming badly worried, fighting back in a struggle for survival. Some of them were ruthless, but stupid. Others were smart. But one single term characterized them all. Ruthlessness was their hallmark.

Tonight, whether by chance or design, the stage was running empty, and they were using it as a convenient means of getting him swiftly out of the Gulch to some less crowded place. There were too many Vigilantes gathering along the gulch.

Well, luck had a way of smirking, coy one day, the next with a knife between its teeth. He'd made the mistake of assuming, as some of the others were doing, that the early hangings had really thrown fear into The Innocents, that the Vigilantes had them on the run and might wind the whole thing up in a hurry; tonight's meeting, he'd figured, would be climactic.

And so it might well be proving, though not as he'd

expected. Maybe he'd pressed his luck too far by not confiding in his fellow Vigilantes quite all he'd known or suspected. The difficulty had been that much was based merely on suspicion, even if in his own mind there had been scant room for doubt.

Perhaps his weakness was due in part to his training. Back in his native Kentucky, he'd read law for a couple of years, being almost ready to stand for admittance to the bar when the war had thrown the world out of kilter. His studies had said that suspicion was one thing, proof another, and that it was bad policy to confuse them.

Yet in these peculiar circumstances, perhaps it was foolish *not* to. He might have enlisted help in his personal crusade, since the ultimate objective was the same. Now it was too late to worry about that. It was likely that his personal affairs and the public welfare were intertwined in tonight's business, and to answer questions, or fail to answer, would change the final result not at all.

The ultimate result in either case would be death. Only the manner of a man's dying might be slow or swift, so that death could come as a friend, eagerly welcomed. The thought was hardly a pleasant one. It tightened his stomach, tying the muscles in knots, scraping the nerves raw like a knife scraping across stretched skin.

The *why* for his being kept alive was clear enough,

and eminently reasonable from his enemy's point of view. In their private business, he possessed answers to questions, answers which were badly wanted.

It was sixty or seventy miles, give or take a few, to the stop at Three Forks. They should make it there before daylight. There would be halts for a change of teams along the way, and there was always the possibility other passengers would be waiting to take the stage. That, however, was unlikely at that season of year. These night runs would soon be discontinued, with winter in the offing. Meanwhile, here he was—

Another wild lurch of the coach flung him to the floor again, this time with his head in the opposite corner. It banged unpleasantly against the edge of the seat, and he lay a few moments, dazed and blinded by pain. Then, sliding with the motion, he became conscious that something was unpleasantly rough against his fettered wrists, and in sudden hope he quested with his fingers.

The roughness wasn't much, merely the point of a nail, or possibly a screw or bolt, thrusting up through the floor, loosened by the stresses and strains of mountain roads. But it represented a chance.

Law worked stubbornly, his jaw clamped against the agony when the shifting and rolling of the vehicle rasped his skin and flesh against the upthrusting iron, in place of the cords twisted about his wrists. Lying double on one's back was not the best position from which to work at a knot, but the painful contusions resulting from the operation were mild by comparison with what he could anticipate at journey's end. Those two words would be precise and accurate as far as he was concerned.

He held his breath, waiting uncertainly, as the stage slowed to a stop and the teams were changed. The cords had loosened a bit, a knot slipping, though not enough to permit him to free either hand. If the driver, or someone else, should look inside now—

No one bothered. Through the cracks, he caught the gleam of a lantern, and the shadows created by it jerked, moving monstrously. The light vanished with the slam of a door, and the stage lurched with renewed motion, flinging him painfully against the side. Law gritted his teeth and kept doggedly at his self-appointed task.

Loosening the knots took longer than he had expected, but finaly he tugged a hand free. It was still a slow job, struggling in the rolling, jolting vehicle to unfasten his ankles, but that too he managed. Now at least he was in a position to make a fight for his life.

5.

Keith mopped the vestiges of fried egg and bacon grease from his plate with a final bite of biscuit, washed plate and cup and stacked them on a shelf from long habit, then let himself out, shivering in the brisk air of dawn. Frost made a white blanket across exposed surfaces, and the leaves which still clung to the cotton-woods were brown and yellow, rustling with an uneasy rasp. Those on hillside bushes flamed as though in defiance against the oncoming winter.

The gulch, for the most part, was still asleep. As usual, it was undisturbed by the latest outrage. Keith's glance traveled to The Golden Promise, and a shadowy figure outlined near its door lifted a hand to scratch solemnly among a thatch of whiskers. That meant that there was no further news, that nothing had been heard of Law or McManus.

Another stage came rolling in, having also traveled through the night, heading east from Bannack. A single paassenger alighted, staggering uncertainly as he set foot on solid earth, his eyes glassy with fatigue. He staggered across to a restaurant and disappeared inside.

Two other men appeared, one a miner, the other with the look of the East still upon him. They took a turn or so to stretch their legs as a fresh team was hooked into place, then, along with Keith, took their places inside, and the journey continued.

They topped a slope, and the sun flamed across the east. As the day wore on, the road sought to follow the Madison, just as, beyond Three Forks, it would trail the Missouri to Fort Benton and the road of navigation. Since neither stream was particularly cooperative, with deep canyons, high mountains and other barriers frequently making travel difficult, the route swerved and twisted and was tortuous for man and beast alike. Yet a road it was, of sorts, with regularly scheduled transportation out from Bannack to the long, bloody gold gulch; thence to Three Forks, and on to the divide called Bird Tail, to Sun River and finally Benton.

The fact that the road remained east of the main range of the Rockies could fool the uninformed. Other ranges, which made up the foothills of the parent mountains, were mighty upthrusts; these had a habit of placing themselves squarely athwart the routes which men wished to travel.

Keith had considered taking a horse and riding

alone, but had decided in favor of the stagecoach. Despite the atmosphere of indifference along the gulch, there were always men who kept a watchful eye on travelers. Those who rode alone, and hastily, were objects of suspicion—and word could outrun the fastest horse.

If Law was ahead, he might well reach Fort Benton ahead of Keith. But there, barring the off-chance of a boat on the verge of taking off for the down-river run, he'd be forced to wait until transportation was available. Not many boats made the run, and few followed a close schedule.

The boats were a link with a forgotten world, another life. Before the ice closed in, the last ones would reach St. Louis or Memphis.

No, not the latter, on the Mississippi. That he thought of Memphis showed the power of habit. River craft no longer journeyed so far south. But up here the war was so remote and far-off that it was all but forgotten.

The first part of the journey was uneventful. It was when they mad a second stop to change teams that news awaited them; new of the man he sought, John Law.

It confirmed the earlier report that Law had been on the night stage. At that stop, apparently without reason or provocation, he had assaulted the driver, taking him by surprise, choking him into submission.

Except for the timely arrival of the stableman, he mght have killed him. Afterward Law had escaped into the darkness.

Beyond that, there was no news. A raw wind was whipping dead leaves from branches, leaving them stark on the chilly ground. Clouds obscured the sky, and the day was gray. The news was about normal.

It was early evening when they pulled in to the station near Three Forks; this marked the end of the night runs. Until the following summer, the stages would travel only by day, lying over through the winter nights. With the imminence of storms and blizzards, night travel was too risky.

No one on board was inclined to quarrel with such a decision. It was tiring enough to ride for a long day, resting at night. The catch was that nighttime accommodations might be almost as unrestful as a jouncy ride through the blackness.

Keith saw the long, low building which furnished accommodations there. There were rooms available, also board, and a bar. Tonight, to the disgruntlement of the extra passengers they had picked up during the day, the bar was not in operation. The landlady made the announcement truculently, glaring out from beneath uncombed gray hair, eyes challenging in a face which might have been improved by soap and water. She wiped reddened hands on a dirty apron.

"Grub's ready, so set up and et——or shut up if you

don't want to! You'll take what there is and like it!"

The first part of the statement was undeniably correct, though all who accepted the invitation appeared to have reservations at the sight of what passed for food. Potatoes had been boiled in their skins and were a soggy mess. Mutton was a greasier, very questionable item, and the biscuits were rock-hard and barely short of moldy. The coffee was a passable imitation of lye.

The miner who had sat beside Keith and nibbled at a plug of tobacco during the day blanched as he eyed the portion set before him. Gamely he sipped the coffee and sampled the glutinous mass which passed for meat, then sighed and pushed back from the table.

"I'm hungry," he announced plaintively. "My belly's been rubbin' my backbone most of the day, till it's near scraped a hole right through. Just the same, I ain't starved enough to down this gosh-awful stuff that disguises itself—and a mighty thin disguise it is—as food. My tongue draws a line at what our old hound dog would only take out and bury—and bury mighty deep."

The landlady returned from the kitchen in time to overhear his remarks. She rested her elbows on the table and glared.

"So you don't like what's set before you, eh?" she demanded. "Well then, starve—and serve you right!"

"Meg, ma'am, I don't know how it'll serve me, but I'll take my chances on starvin'," the miner returned. "Maybe we could run us down a jack rabbit, Keith," he added, "or even a polecat." He seemed unfazed by the glare. Keith, toying unhappily with his own plateful, caught an unexpected gleam in the eyes of the landlady, and wondered.

No one did more than nibble at the food. Keith went outside, tightening his belt a notch. It was dusk by now, and he could do with a bit of walking after the daylong ride.

All day he'd mulled over his assignment, not liking it. But duty was not a matter of personal choice. Burden had been his friend, which in itself was reason enough to hunt down his slayer. And the news indicated that Law was ahead, almost certainly fleeing the country. The evidence seemed clear.

Yet there was something wrong somewhere. He'd liked Law, and so had Burden. Somehow it didn't add up.

The trees grew tall at the side of the halfway house, the night crowding beneath them. As he was about to turn back, he paused at a whispered word, then swung to stare in amazement.

It was the landlady, beckoning from the corner of the house. She was a different woman from the slovenly creature who had shoved that terrible mess at them and ordered them to like it or lump it. The dirty apron had been removed, an application of soap and water made to the face, while a comb run through hair no longer gray had wrought a transformation. Keith caught his breath.

It was something more, of course—here was a subtle magic which dirt and sloppiness had served to disguise. The landlady had appeared to be Meg, a woman well past middle-age, but this girl was young, and he sensed that in better light she might come close to beauty. Yet undeniably she was the same woman.

She placed a finger lightly against full red lips, glancing around uneasily as Keith approached at her gesture. She turned, leading the way deeper into the gloom. Keith hesitated, aware that though the gulch was a day's ride behind, trickery and treachery were everywhere. Then he followed, impelled as much by the mystery as by the fact that she was a woman, and obviously in need of help.

She halted, then, catching the look on his face, smiled, but without humor.

"Don't look so surprised," she said. "I had to fix up that way—how else could I even exist, alone, in such a place?"

Considering her youth, it was a good question. "But you don't belong here," he protested.

"No," she agreed, "I don't. I got here a few hours ahead of you, to find myself alone. I didn't know what to do, so I fixed myself up that way and played the part of Old Meg temporarily. But that man called you Mr. Keith. Are you Harley Keith, from Pine Grove?"

"That's my name, and I've spent the summer there," Keith acknowledged. Her sigh of relief was heartfelt.

"I've heard of you, Mr. Keith—favorably. So I'm appealing to you. If you're on your way to Fort Benton, take me with you—please! It's a matter of life and death!"

6.

Her statement seemed somewhat over-dramatic, and then Keith saw that she was on the verge of tears. There was something strange in this; it might be a trap. But the least that he could do was find out what was going on.

"I'll be glad to help if I can," he agreed. "But I don't understand."

She gave him an uncertain smile, and her face now was winsome and appealing, not at all what it had seemed while she played a part. It occurred to him that she was a good actress in at least one of her roles; perhaps both. But he put the thought from him.

"You poor man," she said suddenly, "I know you're starved. Come inside, and I'll fix you something that's fit to eat. Then we can talk."

Wondering, he circled to the rear, where she let them into the kitchen. In the light of a candle she set out fresh viands upon a kitchen table, which he saw was freshly scrubbed. There were fresh biscuits, hot from the oven, browned to a turn as she ran to it and opened the door. From the oven also came a warmed-over roast, which he judged to be venison, tender and appetizing. Fresh coffee was in the pot. His amazement showed in his face.

"If you can cook like this, why did you serve up that other awful stuff to hungry men?"

"Meg said to do it that way," she explained, and blinked rapidly. "I've been pretending to be her, as she said I should. I didn't like it, but she insisted it was the only way."

Keith ate hungrily, sensing that she would tell the story in her own time and manner. She had a hearty appetite, too, and added no details until they had cleaned their plates. Then she stood up.

"You've been very understanding," she declared gratefully. "Now you may be shocked, but try to understand the rest."

She opened another door. Inside, neatly laid out on her bunk, was Meg. Since her reputation had traveled to the gulch and beyond, Keith had not been surprised at the sort of welcome they had received or the quality of the food.

The gray hair had been neatly combed, but even after such ministrations as had been attempted, she was unmistakably the landlady of the halfway house. A measure of peace had replaced the stress on her face.

Keith saw that the younger woman's disguise had

been remarkably accurate. Even the stage driver, who must have seen Old Meg many times, had failed to notice the difference. Most of the attention had been centered on the messy food, exactly as intended.

"When I arrived here, she was dying," the girl explained. "She was staggering, nearly falling, as she tried to get back inside the house. I did what I could to help, and she was pleased. Poor soul, she's had a hard life and known little enough of goodness or tenderness, I'm afraid. She was grateful, but more worried about what might happen to me than about herself. She told me what to do, and I followed her instructions as well as I could."

Keith's amazement was growing. Death in itself was not unusual. Rather it was almost a commonplace in the land, where life was held more cheaply than gold. It was natural death which was rare. Somehow, seeing the peace which had come to Meg's face, he could feel no regret.

"I'm sure that she had to be rough and hard to exist at all under such conditions," the girl added. "But underneath she possessed a streak of tenderness. She was worried about what might happen to me, not thinking of herself."

"When did it happen?"

"This afternoon. So I warmed up what I found in the kettle in the kitchen. Poor soul, apparently she wasn't much of a cook. I had no clear idea what I'd do afterward, but it seemed best to take one step at a time. Then I heard your name, and since I'd heard of you, Mr. Keith, as an honest man, and trustworthy, I decided to tell you my story. Meg advised me to try to find someone like you. She said that it was dangerous to travel alone."

"She was right," Keith agreed. "You want to reach Fort Benton?"

"I must. I wasn't exaggerating when I said that it may be a matter of life or death. If you will help me, I will be most grateful."

It required no son of a prophet to foresee that there might be complications, but Keith was becoming accustomed to them. In any case, he couldn't refuse.

"I'll help as much as I can," he told her. "Just what did you have in mind?"

"I've been wondering about that," she admitted. "I suppose I'll be rather hard to explain—and so will she. I don't want to embarrass you, or get you into any sort of trouble. And of course some explanation will have to be given—"

They returned to the kitchen, and the empty plates gave Keith an idea.

"Are there any supplies on hand?" he asked. "Enough to prepare a good breakfast for everyone?"

"There's plenty," she agreed. "I looked things over."

"Then how about you cooking a good breakfast for everyone in the morning, as fine a meal as you can manage? Everybody will be ravenous, but not very hopeful, and a good meal will go a long way toward putting them in a co-operative mood. Then maybe we could tell them that you came to look after Meg—that you're her niece, for instance, and that she kept you out of sight in the kitchen."

He shook his head, instantly discovering flaws as he articulated the plan. "No, that would hardly do. The first part, maybe, but not the rest."

He frowned at the thought of further complications, when they should go on with the stage. Meg had known what she was talking about in giving advice to a young woman traveling in that country. If he was to protect her, there would have to be a sound reason for offering that protection. Otherwise they could count on trouble.

"How would it be to say that you came out from the East to marry me?" he asked. "You were on your way to the gulch, due to a misunderstanding, and I was going to meet you. That's it. I didn't meet you as expected, so you were coming to find me, and of course you revealed yourself to me, as you've done, but not immediately. That will give me the right to look after you until we reach Fort Benton. As for Meg—we'll explain that she was taken suddenly sick during the night. We will have to bury her in the morning."

Watching, he saw the rush of color in the girl's pale cheeks, but her eyes remained steady.

"Yes, that would sound like a good reason," she

conceded, "if you don't mind the lie."

"I've told bigger ones for poorer reasons," Keith returned lightly. He was suddenly strangely exhilarated at the prospect. His reasons for journeying to Benton had previously been mixed, but overridingly grim. Now at least they would have a lighter side. "But if I—if we are to pose as being engaged—then I should at least know your name."

"Yes, I suppose you should," she agreed. "You're being very kind to help me, and you deserve to know something about me. I'm anxious to get back to Fort Benton to find my brother, if I can, and help him. I came out from the East—that part is true—but I didn't find him there. Now I hope—I have reason to believe— that he may be at Benton, after all, or on his way there. I'm afraid that he needs help even more than I do. You may have heard of him. He's usually known as John Law. I'm Martha Law."

7.

The months along the gulch had afforded Keith valuable training, both in schooling his emotions and holding his face to a careful blankness, come what might. Even at that, Keith was hard pressed to hide his surprise.

Martha Law! It was no wonder that she had seemed familiar, from the moment when she had called to him from the dusk. John Law had been not only a fellow Vigilante, but his friend. They had worked and planned together and, even in a society where it was not only difficult but dangerous to trust anyone, he had been ready to stake his own life on the integrity of Law. In the broad sense of the term, he had done so.

He had been hit doubly hard by the apparent defection of Law, and then being the one chosen to run him down and execute judgment against him. He had taken on the mission because it appeared that Law had been no real friend, betraying one of the members to his death, if he had not actually been the killer. But this was a situation as monstrous as it was startling.

Now Law was fleeing for his life, and he was going after him, to hunt him and kill him in turn! Of course he intended to make certain that Law was guilty, but there was not much reason for doubt. Law's hasty departure from the gulch, hard on the heels of the grim events there, seemed hardly the act of an innocent man.

This woman whom he had promised to help was John Law's sister—a sister anxious to find her brother so that she might save him from his enemies, from men such as himself!

It made a pretty kettle of fish, and the farther matters went, the more twisted and complex they were likely to become. Ruefully, Keith recognized the pitfalls of the situation. Yet he'd given Martha his promise, and he couldn't go back on it, especially since she was alone and unprotected in such a wilderness. How she had managed thus far he had no idea, but such luck could not be stretched too far.

She might be playing a part, as Law had done; perhaps there was as complete a lack of scruple behind those steady eyes and lovely features as had been the case when he'd been duped, but somehow Keith couldn't believe that. It was more likely that she was ignorant of her brother's real activities, and in no way responsible for his conduct. It had been known even to his friends that Law had a tendency toward wildness, and she probably knew that also and was anxious to restrain him before his conduct led to an unpleasant climax.

"I've met your brother in the mining camps," Keith observed soberly. "But he has left the gulch, and you're probably right about his heading for Benton. Right now, though, we'd better try and get some sleep. Tomorrow will be a hard day, and we'll need to be ready for it."

"Whatever you say," she agreed. "And I want you to know that I'm very grateful, Mr. Keith. I hope that you'll never have cause to regret playing the part of a Good Samaritan. I will do my best to see that you do not."

Her face was troubled, tired from the events of the day, but in the eyes which she turned to him there was such gratitude and tenderness that his convictions were at once strengthened yet shaken. They were strengthened in regard to herself, shaken where Law was concerned. With such a sister, a man could not be a killer.

The trouble with such logic was that it wouldn't wash. Plenty of men from excellent backgrounds had gone bad on the frontier. It was almost fatally easy to justify weak conduct in one's own mind; and one step at a time, if enough of them were taken, could lead all the way downhill.

Keith had doubted his ability to sleep with such matters on his mind, but he awoke as the others around him began to stir. Accommodations at the halfway house consisted of a blanket and a place on the floor of the common room. Keith had endured worse.

The miner was rubbing his eyes, sniffing the air with suspicion and incredulity. Sounds of activity came from the kitchen, from which a fragrance wafted, unmistakably of food; odors not merely appetizing but tantalizing.

"Reckon I'm still dreamin'," the miner asserted doubtfully. "I was havin' a beautiful dream, about food that a man could set his teeth into—stuff like ham an' aigs. Now I can fairly smell the stuff—it seems downright real!"

Keith sat up and reached for his boots. The others were waking as well.

"I guess what you smell is for real boys, and I'll explain," Keith observed. "I've something to tell you—news that's part good and part bad, about what happened last night after the rest of you were asleep. We didn't bother to wake you, for there wasn't a thing that anybody could do."

The stage driver scrubbed a fist raspingly over his unshaven chin.

"Are you intimatin', Keith, that something happened —some sort of a miracle that would teach even Old Meg how to cook?" he asked.

"No miracle," Keith denied. "And we really can't blame Meg too much for what she dished up last night. Under the circumstances, she did pretty well to give us anything, sick as she was."

"Sick?" All the group were regarding him closely, not understanding, yet sensing trouble. "Well, she didn't look too well, for a fact—though when it comes to that, she never does."

"I've a few things to explain, part of them personal," Keith said. "Maybe I'd better start with myself and work up from there. I was going to Benton, aiming to meet a lady there—a little lady who's come clear out from the East to marry me." He was aware of a pause in the activities in the kitchen, but the others were too intent to notice.

He went on, seeing the surprise on every face, but allowing no time for possible remarks.

"With mail service and other transportation the way it is, there was sort of a slip-up. Anyhow, she got to Benton earlier than I had expected, and when she didn't find me there, she started out for the gulch to look for me. She got as far as this place yesterday, riding a horse she'd hired. She found Meg almost flat on her back and did what she could to help her. Meg got to feeling a little better, and you all know how stubborn she was. She insisted on fixing the supper, for she wanted Martha to stay out of sight. Meg told her that it was safer that way, for a young woman alone in this country. Martha hadn't gotten around to telling Meg about me, and when I showed up along with the rest of you, she didn't have a chance to explain right away.

"After supper, about the time you fellows went to sleep, Meg took a turn for the worse. Martha got her into her bed, and then she called me, knowing that Meg needed help. But it was too late. Poor Old Meg had some sort of an attack, and she was dying. Like I say, there wasn't a thing to do, she went that quick, so I didn't bother the rest of you. Before we go on, we'll have to dig a grave and give her a decent burial. As for what you smell, it's Martha's cooking. She's making breakfast for everybody."

He finished tugging on his boot, stood up, crossed to the door of the kitchen and knocked. Martha opened it and appeared in the doorway, smiling shyly. Keith placed an arm about her shoulders, standing beside her to face them.

The effects of the disguise had been completely removed. She looked not only fresh but beautiful, though her eyes showed the trace of tears, and the effect of her beauty and grief on the others was more than sufficient to dissipate any possible doubt or question regarding the story which Keith had told. They were ill at ease, abashed, anxious to be helpful. The news concerning Meg shocked them.

"Pore ol' lady did look kinda peaked, now you mention it," the miner observed. "Guess I was kind of rough in what I said about the grub, too. But I sure didn't mean it that way."

"Well, it was right lucky for Meg, you comin' here the way you did," the driver managed. "Kinda tough for an old lady like her, being sick and alone."

Despite mild regrets, they were able to do full justice to the excellent meal which Martha set before them. Keith's opinion of her cooking rose another notch.

Afterward, in a little open space behind the house, they dug a grave. It was Martha who offered a few words of prayer, while the others removed their hats and watched in silence.

"After all that's happened, we're going on with the stage to Benton," Keith explained, once the brief ceremony was concluded. "I think it's a better town for a lady, with winter coming on."

Heads nodded in solemn agreement. If Fort Benton was something short of a paradise, it was at least an older, more settled community than the towns along the gulch and, by comparison, almost law-abiding. Now the situation had been explained and with Keith as her escort, Martha would receive every respect and courtesy which could be managed.

Keith looked forward to the remainder of the journey with mixed emotions. This was a new role, one which under normal circumstances he would have found pleasant. That was the difficulty. He was in danger of liking it too much, as his acquaintance with John Law's sister ripened. Yet at journey's end she could only hate and despise him.

8.

There had been a time when Law had considered himself a philosopher, fitted to view the world from Olympian heights of calm. Together with other select young gentlemen, he had attended university classes, debating and discussing. In point of actual time, that had not been so very long ago, though now it seemed as far removed in time as it had been from reality.

Now he was sitting, spraddled out in the dust in the middle of a road, clutching a long-barreled Colt's revolver; lifting it only to lower it again, while the stage driver who had occasioned him so much misery whipped up his team and disappeared in a mounting torrent of dust.

It would have been a simple matter, having wrested the gun away, to kill his opponent. Undoubtedly, the circumstances being what they were, shooting the driver would have been a sensible procedure.

The difficulty was that he retained some remnants of philosophy, however frayed and ragged. There was no profit in killing for spite, and certainly no glory in shooting an unarmed man in the back.

What impulse had caused the driver to halt his team and look in on him, there was no way of knowing; perhaps a vague sense of alarm had triggered a response. At any rate, discovery had come before Law was ready. With limbs still stiff and faltering, after being pinioned for hours, he had fought at a disadvantage, been dragged roughly from the coach and tumbled to the road. On the way down he'd gotten a hold on the driver's half-drawn revolver. The fight for possession had been savage.

Law had finally twisted it loose, and in the same moment the untended team had started to run. The driver had sprinted for the stage and made it, then had kept going. Now Law was afoot, and more than ever a wanderer on the face of the earth. Those who had been his enemies were enemies still. Those who had been friends were now enemies.

Getting to his feet, he dusted himself off with slaps of arms which were once more beginning to have a sense of belonging, instead of protruding like wooden appendages clumsily fastened in place. The gun was loaded, and he shoved it into a pocket and considered the situation. Though not entirely sure why he had been kept alive, he could make a reasonably good guess. Certainly the motives of his captors had not been altruistic. Now they would be more determined than ever to destroy him.

The night was worn out, and so was he. Moving as carefully as possible away from the road, he found a place amid the brush and slept.

He awoke, rested but ravenously hungry. The sun was making a final splash across the horizon, and the land gave a deceptive appearance of emptiness.

If his memory served correctly, there was a change station a couple of miles ahead. It would be dangerous to show himself, but he had to have a horse and something to eat. Those who served as custodians would just have to take their chances with a dangerous character.

A light shone yellow against the gloom as he approached the station. There were two buildings, a long, low stable, and the shack which the tender occupied. The one appeared as barn-like and uninviting as the other.

Four horses occupied the stalls in the barn and were contentedly munching hay. Law recognized them as the team which had pulled him the night before. Having been exchanged for a fresh team, and having had a day of rest, one should serve him nicely.

A fragrance of coffee and bacon drifted from the other building. Law sniffed appreciatively and planted his feet in the open door. The coffeepot was boiling, and the big iron skillet was heaped with spuds and bacon. Hot biscuits, invitingly brown, had just been transferred from the Dutch oven to the table. Law saluted softly.

"Howdy, Mart."

Mart Heath was bending above the stove. He clutched the coffeepot in one hand and the skillet in the other, a fortuitous circumstance which rendered it impossible for him to reach for the revolver swinging at his hip. He jerked convulsively, sending a spurt of steaming coffee from the spout, all but losing his hold. His jaw sagged, and as his head turned, his eyes grew glassy.

Law read the hesitation in his mind as to whether to swing and fling the pan and its contents in a desperate effort or submit. The cold eye of the Colt's, looking into his own, decided him. Even as he straightened, his shoulders sagged.

"Now you're being sensible," Law approved. "It would be a shame to waste good grub, specially when we're both hungry." He moved and helped himself to Heath's gun. "Dish things up, two plates. I'm as close to being starved as an old maid to a honeymoon; still, it would be inhospitable to take all a man's supper."

Doubt mingled with suspicion, crawling and twisting behind the tender's narrowed eyes, but he obeyed, dishing the spuds and bacon equally onto tin plates, filling cups with coffee as black as the closing night. His silence had already betrayed him, and this he recognized, making no effort at dissimulation. Whether or not Law was of the brotherhood of The Innocents, in Mart's eyes he was a renegade, deserving no mercy, and to be accorded none.

Law settled into a chair at the table, placing his gun beside the plate. When Heath started to take the other place, he shook his head.

"I can't have you where you might be tempted," he said. "You sit on the floor over there in the corner, with your plate in your lap. Be a shame to waste good grub," he repeated, and the glare faded from Heath's eyes as he accepted the warning.

They ate in silence. Law surveyed the room and found what he wanted: a length of rope coiled and hanging from a peg. Lifting it down, he shook out the loop and approached.

"I know from experience that this sort of treatment is unpleasant," he apologized. "But short of killing you, I don't see any other solution. Put your hands behind your back and hold out your wrists."

Heath started to comply; then rage got the better of him and he made his play, lashing suddenly with one foot. Law lifted his own, kicking hard at Heath's other leg as he surged to his feet. Heath's fall jarred the floor, and Law slapped him with the barrel of the revolver.

"It was your choice," he reminded him, as hate glared from the dazed man's eyes. "I'm obliged to you for a good meal."

He helped himself to Heath's cartridge belt, then, making sure that Heath was securely trussed, puffed out the lamp and let himself out into the night.

He found a saddle horse in the corral behind the barn, and returned to the cabin for a blanket and a supply of grub. Heath watched with mingled fear and malevolence.

"I'll see you hang for this!" he threatened.

"It is comforting to realize that I will have an appreciative audience," Law murmured piously. He reached a decision as he swung to the saddle. He might as well keep on toward Fort Benton, having already covered a sizable portion of the way. He suspected that was the destination they'd had in mind for him, and it would be as good a place as any for a showdown.

There was a light in the halfway house at Three Forks, but he swung wide around it. Some time after midnight, he slept again.

Daylight was mildly disconcerting. He'd saddled the horse in the gloom, working by instinct and experience. When the sun was shining, his pony was revealed as a pinto, but it was too late to make a change. The trouble was that a horse so distinctively marked might attract attention.

It was mid-morning when, from atop a rise, he

sighted another horseman a couple of miles ahead. Blessed with vision to rival an eagle's, Law noted that the horse ahead was also a pinto.

Aside from the two men, the road that day was a lonely one, and would become increasingly so during the unchancy summer. Men who traveled weighed necessity against safety, and whatever answer they arrived at, it was a moot one. None journeyed if they could avoid it.

Sagebrush silvered the landscape, giving the illusion of an inland sea. The gently sloping contours of the land hid Law from the man ahead for the next few miles, except for occasional brief glimpses. Then he heard the distant threat of a rifle. Since the sound came from ahead, Law pulled from the road, keeping to such shelter as was available.

He followed the long break of a gulch, emerging from it to view the road again, and saw the other horse, lying where it had fallen. Its rider had been caught and pinned down. Even as Law saw him, he half-rose up, struggling futilely, then fell back, exhausted.

On every side the land looked empty, but that was no guarantee that the bushwhacker might not still be in the vicinity and watchful. On the other hand, satisfied with his murderous attempt, he might have decamped as hastily as possible.

To show himself was a risk, but Law suspected that he owed something more to the trapped man than the casual gesture of a Good Samaritan. He had a strong hunch that the other pinto might have been mistaken for his own, and that the bullet had been intended for himself.

9.

It was both a boon and a bane to be the most handsome man in any given stretch of territory, whether along the populous Eastern Shore or the scantily occupied reaches of Idaho Territory. Seamus McManus shook his curly blond head and smiled, stroking his waxed mustache complacently. He had never been a man to complain, especially as regarded the gifts of fate. Rather, when matters were not to his liking, he could generally find a way of shifting them to his own purposes.

In such a process, isolated details sometimes had a way of going wrong, but in his own mind McManus was a philosopher. Mistakes—those made by other men—offered an additional challenge to him to offset them. Challenge and excitement were the qualities which made life worth living; they were not the only factors, but they ranked high in importance.

Danger, even acute personal peril, served only to add relish to existence. Playing an exciting game for high stakes would have been enough in itself, but there were always some tempting side dishes, further to whet the appetite.

Such dishes as Martha Law, whom he had first seen a year and a half before, in a setting of moonlight and magnolias. A ball had been in progress, quite as though there had been no such thing as war or its shadow over the land. Only the uniforms of many of the men and the sleek mounts of the officers, tied and chafing at their reins under a great tree, had served as reminders. McManus, attracted by the horses, had been about to help himself to the likeliest of the bunch.

Martha had been outlined in the open door of a stately mansion, framed by candlelight in a soft glow from the room behind, laughing, blushing at the amorous remark of one of the many swains who sighed and languished over her. The rich color in her cheeks had matched the red roses abloom in the gardens at the foot of the steps.

Surrounded and sought after, she had seemed as distant as the moon, just touching the treetops to silver, and as unattainable. Watching, McManus had caught his breath, and in that same moment he had made a resolution that she should one day belong to him. The more impossible a challenge, the more he relished it.

It had required a struggle to make head prevail over heart, to select a horse and ride away, but he'd realized from the start that such a goal would take a lot of doing. His original plan, to get out of the country ahead of those who would stand him in front of a firing squad, had been subtly altered. Much had been accomplished, but much remained to be done.

Remembering, McManus smiled and shook his head. Were his poor mother alive, it would have broken her heart, but she was long past regrets, as he was long past any return along the road he followed. It had been a long trail, and this remote corner of Idaho Territory was a far piece from the old plantation, but attainment was coming closer with each hour.

Half the thrill of the game was in playing a double role. Along the Eastern Shore, before being found out, he'd held commissions in both the armies of the North and the South. Here, it had been his own idea that he should infiltrate the society of the Vigilantes, discovering their secrets for The Innocents, creating confusion and distrust among them. On the whole, his plan had worked well, though it had been a near thing, when he'd discovered that Burden had penetrated his deception and was planning to denounce him at the meeting to be held that same evening.

He'd liked Burden as well as he'd ever liked any man, sensing the loyalty and quiet courage in the coughing, pain-wracked body. It had been a distasteful job to do away with Jim, but necessary. One of them had to die, and when verities were reduced to stark essentials, it always had to be the other fellow.

It had been a fortuitous chance that he had been able almost at once to involve John Law and cause the evidence to point in his direction. Now Law was on his way to Fort Benton, being shipped like so much baggage, whether he would or no. He didn't realize, of course, that he owed his life to his status as the brother of Martha Law.

Sooner or later, Law inevitably would have to die. But for the present he might be more useful alive.

McManus flexed his muscles, fingering the biceps of one arm admiringly. Some men were so musclebound that the best they could ever hope for was to swing a pick and shovel. By contrast, his own body was lean and supple, and few people guessed the extraordinary power so smoothly concealed. Burden, for instance, despite his racking cough, had been appropriately named. Despite that, McManus had managed the hanging by himself, although it was a task which normally would have proved an onerous chore for three men.

Good looks were a problem as well as a gift. It was not easy to lose himself, even amid a crowd. McManus shrugged and smiled, knowing that he'd have had it no other way.

One other matter was a problem. The money belt which he wore concealed about his waist bulged with gold, and even for a man as strong as himself it was by way of being a burden. Still it was a welcome weight, as well as necessary; it represented his share of the many crimes charged against The Innocents during the past half-year.

Most of the outlaws lost their money as fast as they acquired it. There were plenty of ways to spend money in and around the fabulous gulch. In that, The Innocents differed little from their arch-foes the Vigilantes, or the reasonably law-abiding stratum between. With most it was easy come, easy go. Half enviously, half scornfully, he'd watched Bill Fairweather ride up and down the long main street of Virginia City, flinging nuggets to right and left, laughing like a fool as men scrambled in the dust for the largesse. Fairweather, as one of the original discoverers of the golden horde, could easily convince himself that there was no end to the gold, or to the luck of Bill Fairweather.

McManus had not demeaned himself by the scramble for wealth. There were other ways of acquiring gold, and what he got, he hung onto.

His companions had taken note of the fact that he rarely spent much, and he was aware that his cabin had been ransacked on at least a couple of occasions. The only safe place for gold was on one's own person. There, if a man had quickness of wit and sureness of aim, it was protected.

He'd had to kill a couple of his friends, men not so innocent as they seemed, who had tried to take it from him. The word had spread, and among the outlaws he was held in respect, if not in esteem.

McManus shrugged the recollection aside, like a dog shaking itself after emerging from water. Men who made foolish miscalculations deserved to die.

Luck, McManus had found, was like everything else: for the most part you made your own. It came as a shock to him to learn that Law had escaped. Questioning elicited the time and place, and consideration of the obvious indicated what course Law would follow, even to the color of the pony he would be riding on. Having passed that way brief hours before, McManus knew what was available.

To another of the outlaw fellowship he delegated the task of stopping Law, stipulating only that he should not be injured unduly, if that could be avoided. McManus preferred to attend to such things himself, but some chores had to be left to others.

The man who had been caught and pinned down by the dead horse did not appear to be seriously injured. As Law dismounted, he saw that the man's eyes were open, and he studied Law's pinto with speculative interest.

"I sort of wondered why anybody'd shoot at me—and couldn't think of no good reason why they should," he observed as Law dismounted.

"A lot of folks in this country have itchy trigger fingers," Law returned. "But it's possible that they made a mistake in ponies. It's too bad that you didn't have time to jump free."

"I'm some short of being a second cousin to a grass-hopper," the prisoned man explained almost apologetically, "though my lack of spryness works both ways. This peg is wooden, which plumb curtails any cavortin' on my part. On the other hand, the original leg would sure have been in bad shape."

He lay, pinned by his right leg, with the weight of the dead horse resting heavily upon it. Despite his light tone, his face was gray and drawn.

"The first thing is to get you out of there," Law returned, and set to work. He took a rope from his own saddle, looping it about the under rear leg of the dead horse. With the other end attached to his saddlehorn, it was an easy matter to tip the weight off the trapped man.

The man was sitting up, examining the wooden leg, as Law reclaimed his rope. Apparently it had suffered no damage, and he struggled erect, testing his weight on it, striving to grin gamely. The grin became a painful grimace, and he collapsed suddenly, then was motionless as Law bent over him.

Apparently he'd been more seriously hurt than he had guessed. Following that final distressed flutter, his heart had ceased to beat.

Law made sure of that, then straightened, appalled. He probably owed his life to this man, and the fact that he too had been riding a pinto pony. The color of the horse had been the sole means of identification; the bushwhack bullet had been fired at long range.

It was ugly business, but there was nothing more that he could do there. Now, more than ever, his own errand was vital. Fighting a sick dismay, he mounted and rode on.

A shout startled him. Looking back, he saw another horseman approaching the dead pair. The sunlight slanted along a rifle barrel being jerked from its saddle sheath and raised. Law hesitated, torn between impulses. This time he was really hooked on the horns of a dilemma.

The new arrival had probably seen just enough to jump to a reasonably logical, if wholly inaccurate conclusion. Now he was shouting Law's name, demanding that he halt and return. He was a stranger to Law, but Law, unfortunately, was known to him.

Dust rolled in a spreading ribbon on the road behind. The Benton-bound stage was coming into sight.

The newcomer drew his own conclusions and decided the issue. Flame spat redly from the rifle's mouth, and the bullet burned the rump of Law's pinto. It ran wildly, and Law was as thankful as the cayuse that a turn in the road and covering trees were close at hand, as the other man emptied his rifle.

Those on the stage glimpsed the fleeing horseman, while the rifle thundered. The driver pulled up, and the belated witness furnished such details as he knew or suspected.

"It's a clear case o f cold-blooded murder," he growled. "But I got a look at the man that done it. He was bendin' over him, till he saw me coming. Then he took off like a gopher, two jumps ahead of a weasel. Feller from the gulch, name of Law. John Law."

Martha did not cry out, but Keith felt her cringe and shrink. He put an arm about her shoulder, and she trembled against him, seeking reassurance. And the worst of it was that he had none to give.

10.

Had McManus been a cat, he would have been purring as he came to the sprawling environs of what was known as Montana City. Like other gold camps, it had little form or pattern. The main workings followed proven ground, but other men, always seeking and ever hopeful, probed the earth wherever chance or guess indicated. Cabins and tents followed the same haphazard system. Taken in its entirety, Montana City was considerable of a camp, yet somehow as lonely and lonesome as a coyote wailing from a hilltop.

McManus had good reason for satisfaction. No one had interfered with his flight toward the distant town on the river, and he was taking sensible precautions to make sure that no one should.

A tall clump of service-berry brush grew near the rim of the diggings. Warped brown leaves still clung to the branches, and the wood showed a pale blue hue in the last of the sunset. Sheltered from possible observation, McManus delved into his saddle-bags, drawing forth a wrinkled coat and a hat which was battered and the worse for wear. These he substituted for the ones he had been wearing, transferring them in turn to the bags.

The change subtly altered his appearance, but, more to the point, the hat and coat which Law had been wearing when struck down at the gulch were distinctive in pattern, known to many men, and readily recognizable as Law's. Since in build and general physical appearance they were similar, McManus calculated that the effect, especially in the dusk, might be deceptive.

There was a certain risk in wearing Law's garments, but McManus had calculated it carefully. While he wore them, he planned to be seen only at a distance, or in uncertain light. Moreover, the word of Law's latest adventures along the trail would not be known in Montana City.

For a brief time, the strike there had been touted as one to rival the diggings at Alder and in the Tobacco Roots. The early promise had faded, though most men could make wages with a hard day's work, and a few grew rich. It was a camp where men came and went, even more restless than most of their kind. Hastily worked claims might be abandoned overnight, left for any others foolish or venturesome enough to bother with them.

This custom had proved a mild bonanza for some miners whose skin reflected the hue of the metal they sought. As eager for gold as their white cousins, they perforce had to be content, under a six-gun society, to do most of their delving in worked-over and abandoned ground. Out of such doubtful soil, by dint of patience and hard work, many of the Chinese were extracting good wages.

Aware of this, McManus was tolerantly unmindful of the lowering of the standards of society. If the regular men of Montana did not object to the heathen Chinee, as long as they kept in a lowly place, he saw no reason for personal displeasure.

Emerging from the brush, he went on, picking an uncertain trail. Here the ground had been mined and remined until it presented the appearance of a prairie-dog town. This was the section where the wearers of pigtails had largely taken over.

Somewhat to McManus' surprise, there was an appearance of desertion, with very few men of any color of skin at work. It was close to dusk, but most men worked as long as the light held, especially when racing the oncoming winter, which would impose drastic limitations of its own.

Then he understood. This was Saturday evening, and it was an ancient and hallowed custom with most white men to quit work a little early on Saturday, so as to do a bit of celebrating on the town. At the moment, it was a tradition with which McManus found no quarrel.

Such an hour, as he had long since discovered, was

always rich with potential opportunity.

There was always some individual, thriftier, harder-working than the rest, who lingered after the crowd had departed. The nearby hills rose high and wooded, wrapped in their own shadows. The creek, winding down from the mountains, used and re-used for washings of many sorts, wound and twisted through tortuous channels, its ages-old pristine clearness and purity only a memory.

Kneeling beside the stream, hidden except for the top of his head by the pit in which he worked, was a Chinese. The ancient dark brown hat atop his head resembled a brown leghorn hen perched on its nest, and his pigtail bobbed betrayingly with the motion of arms and shoulders. Thus, though his back was toward McManus, he was certain that the miner was an Oriental.

He was very busy washing a final pan of gravel, carefully picking a small spoonful of color from the bottom, stuffing that in turn into a canvas poke. McManus noted with interest that the poke bulged, well-filled and clearly heavy.

Aside from this one man, the diggings had a deserted air. Dismounting carefully, McManus took one quick look around for confirmation, then picked up a stone the size of his fist and threw, hard and accurately.

He'd always prided himself on his aim. When he had been a boy, the family larder had never been plentiful, and powder, though cheap, had been scarce and not to be wasted. He'd trained himself so that he could knock a squirrel off a high limb with a rock, and the skill remained.

The unsuspecting Celestial pitched forward on his face, uttering no outcry. Blood oozed slowly from the scarcely broken skin at the back of the head, staining the black hairs where they started to merge into the braided pigtail.

A few particles of gold spilled from the poke as it dropped from a hand suddenly nerveless. McManus scooped up what had been dropped, drawing the string. It was uncomfortably heavy as he stuffed it into a coat pocket.

He moved without undue haste to a new location, well away from his victim, before halting again. Then, because the poke was unhandy as well as heavy and might be dangerous evidence, he emptied it into his money-belt, then discarded the empty sack. As he went on, the weight about his middle was on the verge of becoming a burden, albeit a pleasant one.

He was still on the outskirts of the camp when the scene was roughly repeated. This time it was a white man who had lingered after most of his fellows had quit work, and he too had a poke, into which he was inserting nuggets. McManus' eyes took on a gleam, as much from amazement as from avarice. Clearly the prospector had enjoyed a rare bit of luck that day, luck such as the gold seeker dreams of but rarely finds.

Routinely washing gravel, he must have stuck his shovel into a pocket at the roots of a clump of brush—a pocket collected by some whim of nature, lying undisturbed through countless thousands of years, unsuspected until that moment. Cannily controlling his excitement, the finder had cleaned out the pocket during the day.

The nest had been cleaned up without attracting attention, which in itself was excellent luck. McManus shook his head in wonderment. His was turning into such a run as he'd seldom enjoyed.

He employed another stone, thrown as before, and again his aim proved accurate. This time, however, his luck turned chancy. The man, falling as the Chinese had done, cried out sharply as he collapsed.

At the sound, McManus dropped with equal celerity to his hands and knees in the shelter of a nearby excavation. He crouched, listening and watching. If no one had heard, all would be well. He was on fire, with fever in his blood—gold fever, the most virulent known to man, in whose name mountains and wildernesses had been explored, new continents opened and all manner of crimes committed. Sight of such a horde of gleamingly fresh nuggets was more powerful than strong liquor.

But it never paid to grow so excited as to lose his head or discard caution. The rule had not only been profitable, but on more than one occasion it had saved him from disaster.

It was still effective. McManus heard the scrambling crunch of boots on gravel; then a voice called, questioning and anxious. Someone had been close enough to hear the cry and was responding. McManus crouched lower, holding his breath. His hand moved tentatively toward his hidden shoulder gun, then shifted to another stone of convenient size. A stone was deadly at close range, and silent.

The other man came in sight. He peered questioningly, saw the fallen man and hurried to him. McManus hesitated, torn between avarice and caution. Prudence dictated that he get away while he could, before an alarm was raised. But the poke of newly mined nuggets held him like an anchor.

The light was failing, as dusk poured like sooty fog across the valley, coming with a softly deceptive air which seemed to ridicule the notion that winter lurked behind the hills. This air was straight out of midsummer, as full of false promise as the pocket of gold had turned out to be.

It was light enough for McManus to recognize the newcomer. He'd met him a couple of times during the summer, once at a conference in Alder Gulch and again at a halfway point between the two camps. Tom Armington was also a Vigilante.

Unlike McManus, he was sincere in the effort to bring law and order to that lawless land. It would never occur to him to play a double game.

Armington stared for an instant at the fallen man, then looked quickly about. He seemed to be torn between the impulses to make a search for whoever was responsible for such an outrage and the impulse to lend aid to the injured. Friendship, and the deepening gloom, decided him. A search would be difficult, probably fruitless. Clearly the man who had cried out needed help, and that as fast as it could be given.

Tom dropped on his knees beside him, then saw the dropped poke, the spilled nuggets. McManus heard his sharp intake of breath, saw the eagerness spread over his face. Understanding came to Armington, as it had come to McManus.

But their reactions differed. Armington turned to the injured man, examining the lump which was beginning to puff against his skull, picking up the stone which had fallen nearby, and correctly assessing that it was the weapon. Again he rose up, this time on his knees, and looked suspiciously around, one hand resting on his gun butt. But there was nothing to see. Then the injured man groaned.

Armington turned back to help, assisting him to sit up, quesioning him as to what had happened. Sick and groggy, the miner could tell little. He tried, with Armington's help, to get to his feet, but fell back with a groan.

"Better let me rest a spell, Tom," he managed. "I

just ain't up to moving—not for a spell."

"You need a doctor," Armington decided. "I'll go bring Snead. You wait while I fetch him."

"I'll wait, all right," the other man agreed. "But you better take this poke, Tom. I found these nuggets —and I'll be easier in my mind if you watch 'em for me till I can see straight again."

"Might be safer for you if I did," Armington acknowledged. He asked no questions regarding the strike, but gathered up the spilled gold, then stuffed the poke into a coat pocket. His face remained anxious.

"I'll be as quick as I can. You think you can make out?"

"Sure. All I need is to rest a spell. And there'll be no reason for anybody to bother me now. It's you who'll need to keep your wits about you, Tom."

"I'll aim to do just that," Armington assured him grimly. "I'd sure like to get a line on whoever did this—preferably along the sights of my revolver!"

"Not much chance of finding out," the injured man sighed resignedly, "unless he's around and tries to get you."

"He'd better do a good job for the first time," Armington swore, and set off. From the distance came a muted but slowly swelling sound in the night. Having heard similar noises many times, McManus recognized it as the voice of the town, awakening to a roaring weekend of celebration. It would swell, and continue through much of the darkness, punctuated, in all probability, at least once or twice by gunshots, before a new dawn ushered in a false Sabbath calm.

Closer at hand the silence was almost total. Birds had departed for a sunnier clime, and animals moved cautiously, venturing on nightly forays where only the craftiest survived. Having no further interest in the man who had found the gold, McManus returned to his horse. Circling, he followed Armington, partly from sound, partly by a fairly sure knowledge of where he had to head.

McManus was tempted to intercept him, to try a sudden silent assault, but caution again prevailed. Tom Armington was alert and on guard, and he was a formidable opponent. This needed to be carefully planned.

A livery stable proclaimed its location by a fragrance not too subtle, yet not too different from many other stenches which seemed to cluster over a mining camp like flies on a screen door. McManus swung down from the saddle, gave brief instructions for the care of his horse and moved forward on foot.

He heard a patter of booted steps, and recognized Armington as he slid through a patch of light, while a door opened and closed. It was luck to find him so readily after losing him. McManus fell into step, far enough to the rear to attract no attention.

A clapboard saloon was ahead, beginning to bustle

with activity. It appeared to be already crowded. Armington turned in, and McManus was not far behind.

At the bar, Armington was inquiring for the doctor. Normally, it seemed, he could be found there most of the time. This night, however, he was not in. The bartender shook his head regretfully.

"Ain't seen him all afternoon, Tom. Don't know where he might be. I'll tell him you were lookin' for him, though, in case he does show up."

"You do that," Armington agreed shortly. "He's needed." He hesitated, then went back outside, intent on making further inquiries. McManus again assumed the part of a shadow.

He was taken off-guard when Armington paused abruptly in his swinging stride and swung about. Here, at another saloon, the proprietor had been somewhat of an innovator, building a small cubicle to overhang the sidewalk, roofed against the weather. In that alcove hung a lantern. Its rays were shed above the door, though it had little effect on the otherwise black cavern of street. They came face to face in the patch of light, both halting.

Apparently Armington had decided to have a look in this place also, and this had caused him to change course so suddenly. He stared, then thrust out a hand.

"Law!" he ejaculated, then hesitated, peering more carefully. His tone changed, held an inflection of surprise. "McManus! I thought at first you were John Law!"

"Why, how are you, Tom?" McManus gripped the proffered hand heartily. "Where'd you come from?"

His heartiness did not dispel the suspicion which had leaped to Armington's face. His eyes were dark with doubt as they ranged over the coat and hat.

"I'd have sworn you were Law," he grunted. "Those sure look like his clothes."

Tardily, McManus remembered that he had forgotten to change back to his own hat and coat, and now it was too late. These garments of Law's *were* distinctive—so damnably so that it would require a really convincing explanation to satisfy Armington as to why he was wearing them. At the moment he could think of nothing which was likely to suffice.

There was another argument which was always potent, however, and he brought his gun muzzle against Armington's back as they moved a step and were in the shadows again. The jabbing pressure caught the Vigilante by surprise. Fortunately, the dark street seemed empty except for themselves.

"Keep your voice down, Man," McManus warned. "I'll explain, all in good time. Why don't we take a bit of a walk and talk matters over? There are several things I need to discuss with you and some of the others. That's why I'm here."

His tone was persuasive, and the gun still more so.

Armington hesitated, clearly not liking it, but he knew better than to argue with a gun, especially when the other man had the drop. Moreover, both Law and McManus were members of the Vigilante group, so there might be a reasonable explanation.

"If you say so," he agreed. "But is the gun necessary?"

"Not if you're in a reasonable frame of mind," McManus responded with disarming readiness, and returned it to a pocket. "I guess my nerves are a bit jumpy, Tom. And after what's happened to Law—not to mention other things—maybe you'll agree that they have a right to be."

"I know what you mean," Armington said. "The Innocents are striking back—and there's a devil of a lot going on. I don't know about Law, but you can tell me. Where are we going?"

"Just to confer a bit, out in the open where no one will overhear," McManus assured him. "It's safer that way."

"I need to find the doctor—a man's been hurt."

"Fine. Where is he likely to be?"

"That's the trouble. He's almost always hanging around Barney's Place, half-soused. Now nobody has seen him."

"In that case, we will keep an eye out as we talk." McManus had been veering away from the busy section. The moon was rising, beginning to shed a faint light. They paused, and Armington looked about uneasily.

"The boys hung a man from that tree the other evening," he muttered. "Now what was it that you had to tell me, McManus?"

"Why, chiefly that I want you to hand over that poke," McManus explained gently. And having allayed suspicion, he struck, clubbing with the long barrel of his Colt's. That made three times he'd used a soundless weapon on a man's head in one evening. This time, like the first, he made certain that no additional blow would be needed.

Armington slumped, making no outcry. McManus found the poke and transferred it to his own pocket, grunting at the weight. Then he made himself one with the shadows.

11.

Dust puffed up from hoofs and wheels, enveloping the stage in a constant gritty cloud, pursuing like nemesis. It penetrated cracks in the floor as well as around the doors, adding to the jolting discomfort which the long leather thorough braces on which the body of the stage was slung did little to alleviate. Once a certain speed was attained and held, the leather, serving in lieu of springs, had a habit of setting up a swaying, relentless motion which made some passengers seasick.

Keith rode, barely aware of surface annoyances, his mind churning with the sudden implications of a wholly unexpected situation.

He had set out from the gulch to do a job, however distasteful. The task remained, more unpleasant than ever, but now he was also acting a part, and all at once reality and make-believe were one and the same.

It was against all rules of good sense to lose his head over a woman—particularly when she was sister to the man whom he was under orders to find and execute. He stared unseeingly out the window, doubting and bewildered, yet caught up in something bigger, more powerful than himself.

The trouble, as with man from the misty beginnings of time, was that Martha was a woman, defenseless and appealing, and she had turned to him for help. It was supposed to be a purely rational alliance, due to last for the duration of this journey to Fort Benton, and no more. He had intended to hold fast to that arrangement, with no thought of sentiment.

Yet somewhere along the way, reason and common sense had been pushed aside. Martha, huddled disconsolately in a corner of the jolting vehicle, riding uncomplainingly, cried out to him more loudly than words could have done. Though she made no sound, no fuss, Keith realized that she was crying.

That was scarcely to be wondered at. It had been a shattering experience to reach Three Forks, as she had done, to find Old Meg dying. The burial, conducted while the chill of dawn was still in the air, had certainly tugged at her sympathy, as it had at the heartstrings of the company of strangers who were the only mourners. The rest of them had stood about, abashed and uncertain. Old Meg's reputation in the territory had been almost as fearsome as that of some of the outlaws.

Dead, Meg had again become a woman, and the

realities of the long trail were suddenly frightening.

Martha had been the only one composed enough or with the wit to act. She had offered a prayer. Any petition to a higher power must have rung strangely in the ears of the group, but Keith had been the only one to sense the effort which it required of a young woman among strangers to offer up such a word in public. Her earnest simplicity had impressed them all.

It had affected Keith, making him proud of her yet humble, so confused that he was having a hard time sorting out his feelings. His impulse as well as his desire was to take her in his arms, to comfort her. How was a man supposed to comport himself, under such circumstances?

Self-consciousness had kept him aloof for the first few miles after the stage got under way, while he tried hard-headedly to face facts. As far as these others knew, she had come out to that country to marry him; therefore a reasonable display of emotion should not be amiss. On the other hand, this was a public conveyance, and he could not forget that it was only a business arrangement, and they were virtual strangers. He sat awkward and silent, while the other occupants of the coach looked uncomfortable.

The stage slid to a sudden halt in a thickening cloud of dust, amid startled exclamations by the outside passenger and profane comments by the driver, directed to his suddenly skittish team. Keith caught a glimpse of a figure beside the road, a dead horse sprawled close by, and tried to get between the sight and Martha. But she had already seen.

They alighted, and became aware of another man on the scene. He had emptied his gun after the supposed killer only minutes before. Now he was bluntly graphic in his description of what had taken place.

"It was as cold-blooded a killing as ever I've seen," he growled. "I was riding off west there when it happened. Hearin' the shooting, I headed this way. I come up in time to see the murderin' hound. He was bendin' over this poor devil, but as soon as I came in sight, he took off mighty fast. I tried to stop him, but it was kind of far, and I guess I missed the so-and-so—"

His eyes fixed upon Martha, widening incredulously as he became aware that there was a woman in the party. He jerked off his hat, almost choking with wrath and confusion.

"Beggin' your pardon, ma'am, but I didn't realize there was a lady present. Just the same, I'm sorry I missed the murderin' good-for-nothing. Like I say, he took off mighty fast when he saw me, but not quite fast enough. I managed to get a good look at him."

The driver asked the question. "Anybody you knew?"

"Sure was. He comes from the gulch—that bloody gulch that's gettin' to be a hang-out for all the riffraff of half a continent. Feller name of Law. John Law."

Martha tensed, her already white face losing such vestiges of color as had remained. Understanding, Keith set an arm about her shoulders, but none of the others took any particular note. For a moment Keith feared that she might faint; then he realized admiringly that in such a crisis she could be rock-like. It had taken more than impulse to reach that point on a wilderness journey.

His own mind rejected the implication of what the witness was saying almost as violently as hers. Such a murder, by law, was too monstrous, too senseless.

Yet that was an almost perfect description of half the crimes committed by The Innocents. They killed wantonly, without reason, and he had long since suspected that it was their purpose to heighten a reign of terror, to frighten any who otherwise might find courage to resist. Thus, if this slain man had tried to stop Law, recognizing him as one of The Innocents, a fugitive—

The terrifying part was that the unthinkable was logical.

There was more delay, while they dug another grave, a few steps back from the road. It would take too long and be too difficult to inform the law before taking such direct and necessary action. And the law was Henry Plummer, a mockery of a lawman.

Some of the others glanced questioningly at Martha

as they prepared to lower the victim into the soil which would be his final shroud. She stared stonily, giving no sign of emotion. Only Keith understood, and he could neither explain nor give any outward indication. To her this was personal, a worse tragedy than any of them suspected.

His mind was churning as they resumed the journey. The positive identification of Law as the murderer, together with the unchancy chain of events, left him angry and bewildered. He'd counted Law not only as a fellow Vigilante, but as a friend. The killing back at the gulch had shaken him badly. For that one, however, there was an explanation, a reason, rooted in self-preservation. So senseless a killing as this lacked even that excuse.

There was one difference as the stage went on. The other passengers had chosen to ride on top, finding somewhat elaborate if clumsy excuses to leave Martha and Keith to themselves. They were not insensitive to the girl's shocked reaction to two deaths in a row, and were taking this method of expressing their sympathy, affording her such privacy as was possible.

She dabbed furtively at her eyes with the edge of a small, frilly handkerchief. Despite her grief, her profile was wistfully appealing. Keith's indecision vanished. As at the graveside, he placed an arm about her shoulders. That much he had intended, as a gesture of comfort. It was his own words which surprised him.

"I don't believe it!" he declared passionately, though he kept his voice low, so that it would be inaudible to those on the outside. "Your brother's not that sort, Martha. Something mighty strange is going on around here. He wouldn't do a thing like that, and if he did find it necessary to shoot, he wouldn't run like a scared coyote. He's not the running kind!"

He almost convinced himself, the words reminding him anew of what he had learned about John Law. During the summer, there had been at least two occasions when danger had been real and imminent; each time discretion, as well as common sense, had indicated retreat as a logical course. Others had even set the example.

Not John Law. He'd stubbornly refused to back a step.

Martha turned her head, studying his face gravely. Her swimming eyes were grateful.

"I know he couldn't have done such a thing," she agreed. "John would never stoop to such a cowardly act. The awful part is that others should think so! Now, when this story is spread around, he will be branded an outlaw, hounded and pursued."

"With that other fellow jumping to conclusions the way he did, shooting at him first, of course he didn't have any chance to explain," Keith added. "Providing it was him to start with, because there could have been a mistake. The trouble with this country," he concluded tiredly, "is that nobody trusts anyone else."

Martha snuggled closer to him. "I don't know what I'd do without you," she whispered. "It's almost as though I *had* come out to meet you. You're so kind and understanding."

With daylight and renewed activity, Montana City was buzzing like a kicked-over ant hill, a situation not only of his creation but eminently to the liking of McManus. In such an atmosphere he walked as he pleased, unsuspected, largely unnoticed, the moving force among a horde of ant-like creatures. Blindly unreasoning, they deserved no better of life than they usually received. Thinking thus, he was both amused and contemptuous.

What was more to the point, certain others, who also shrouded themselves in the cloak of innocence, were quick to bring him word; he had always been a leader, so they kept him informed of news which was either interesting or very possibly pertinent.

Even they did not guess that he was concerned in this latest crime wave which had rocked the camp. Another piece of news had reached him during the shank of the evening, brought by a man on horseback; news which did concern him. John Law had escaped the trap set for him; another and innocent man had fallen victim, due to the chance that he had ridden a horse with similar markings to Law's mount.

That was something to note and guard against, since Law, though now a fair target for any man's gun, was still at large. And Law was always dangerous.

Equally pertinent was the chance report concerning the stagecoach and its passengers. Outwardly, McManus heard with no visible interest. Inwardly, he was shaken. Martha was on the stage, and heading that way—her ultimate goal probably the same as his own: to reach Fort Benton.

That she should have made the hazardous journey west was surprising, and that she had gotten so far inland from the river even more so. Now that she had done so, the situation was fraught with possibilities.

The news that Harley Keith was on the same stage, and that Martha had come west to marry him, was even more surprising, and scarcely as pleasant.

There was a mystery here, since that part of the story could hardly be so. Not that it mattered, except that it added another count against Keith.

Since Keith was on the stage, not yet stopped, he was becoming a menace. It was high time to dispose of him.

The delays along the way had again ruined the stage's schedule. It had been supposed to reach Montana City for the next night's rest. Instead, McManus was informed, it had pulled in at a ranch house a dozen miles short of the camp.

Having pondered these items, McManus acted with

characteristic dispatch. He confided certain of his plans and desires to two men of disreputable appearance but reasonable trustworthiness.

"You're to meet the stage in the morning," he instructed them, "soon after it starts again, and as far as possible short of the camp. Throw down on the driver and stop it. I don't care what happens to him, or to any of the passengers, one way or another. But make sure of two things. One is, you're to kill Keith. The other is that the woman is not to be hurt. Bring her to me—and I'll have a thousand dollars in nuggets for each of you for your day's work!"

12.

The cluster of buildings known as Illman's Ranch were set a comfortable distance back from the road, hidden from sight by hills and trees. These insured a privacy which the owner found desirable. The ranch was mildly prosperous, despite the problems posed by the finding of gold at nearby Montana City and other more strident camps within the territory, and by the questionable quality of the citizenry. Employees had a tendency to quite without warning, to try their luck at the camps. Guests, rarely invited but never turned away, whether they came for a meal or for a night, ran a wide gamut both as to character and integrity.

Illman had solved most of his problems. Possessing the build for that sort of thing, he had tried digging for gold, discovering for himself that it was hard work; also that he was of that large company whose luck was nothing to crow about.

Taking part in wide-ranging stampedes, he had been impressed by the immensity of the open range, land for the taking, ignored by most. Also, there was an unending multitude of travelers, both into and through the country. Many of these drove ox teams; the animals were usually gaunt and footsore by the time the gold country was reached. Most of the drovers were short alike of rations and of cash.

Taking his pick of the land, Illman had found it not only to his liking but profitable to trade for cattle, to fatten them on his grass, then to sell the better ones for fresh service in the yoke. The others were readily bought by butchers at the various camps. As for his guests, he treated all alike, asking no questions, enforcing only one demand—that in return for hospitality they leave behind feuds and grudges while at the ranch.

The stagecoach and its passengers were received in that spirit. Though no more than a dozen miles separated them from the gold camp, it was not so short a distance as it sounded, or an easy road for travel by night. By day, the less said about it the better, in the opinion of those who traversed it.

The coach's load was considerably lightened when they set out the next morning. Either the other passengers had reached their destination, or had changed their minds and, securing horses from Illman, proceeded independently. Keith and Martha were the only passengers when they again took to the road.

Keith frowned as he stepped inside and closed the door. This might be chance, or it could mean something else. Prairie-chickens had a way of scattering in the grass and vanishing like shadows at the threat of a hawk. Nor were they alone in scenting danger and acting to forestall it.

Unostentatiously, he placed himself so that he could reach his holstered gun quickly and without hindrance.

The precaution paid off almost as soon as they returned to the main road. A clump of cottonwoods grew close at hand. Unlike many of their fellows, these retained their leaves, brown and yellow but making a good cover. Out from these, without warning, rode a pair of masked men, each with a rifle held at the ready. The shouted command to pull up and to be quick about it was so truculent that it bordered on the savage.

That harshness was their undoing. The driver had had more than sufficient experience under similar circumstances to appreciate the folly of resistance. He started to obey, but the mien and tone of the nearer outlaw spooked the lead horse closest to him. A cayuse by inheritance as well as training, it closed its teeth on the bit and plunged ahead, forcing its teammates to a sudden run.

The masked pair reacted with a savagery to match their voices. A rifle blasted, and the driver pitched over the side and to the road, there to lie sprawled, his part in the drama concluded before it was well begun.

Keith's reaction was prompt. The command to halt did not surprise him, and the possible reasons for the holdup were clear in his mind. It might be that the outlaws suspected the stage of carrying gold from the gulch, and that their sole interest lay in that. That was an unlikely possibility, since prudent men rarely entrusted gold to the express. The absence of a shotgun guard would have convinced experienced road agents that the coach carried nothing of value.

It might well be he himself whom they sought; an attack would be the best defense. In any case, their cold-blooded shooting of the driver was reason enough for retaliation.

Keith had the door open a crack. Holding it with one hand, he emptied his revolver with the other, shooting with swift precision. The wild lurching of the stage was no particular handicap, for he had trained himself to shoot under still more difficult conditions.

He was unable to determine just how effective his fire was, for one rider dropped quickly out of view, whether from fright or because he could no longer retain a seat in the saddle was a matter for conjecture. The second raider, who had bellowed the command, came on with a savage thrust of spurs, then swung about and rode blindly away. Keith judged that his grasp upon the reins was frenzied but unthinking, as blood spattered to mark his trail.

Martha, whose face had again been pleasantly vivid, was pale but composed. She made no effort to grab Keith or to scream or otherwise to hamper him, and for that he was grateful. It was abruptly apparent that the danger, far from being over, was only beginning. The horses were running away, frenzied with terror, no hand now on the reins, which were flapping and whipping about their hoofs, adding to their fear.

For a short distance the road was good, twin wheel traces across an easy sea of grass. It was not a condition that would last long enough for them to tire from running. After half a mile or so, it became a narrow, crooked trail, twisting among hills, with disaster looming at either side.

"Hang tight," Keith adjured, and with the door wide, reached and got a grip on the edge of the driver's seat above. He swung out, teetering in space, his muscles cracking with the strain. Then he managed to pull himself up, to get an arm resting over the top, and then to flounder up.

It was barely a beginning, and of doubtful value. He twisted, got his foot against the brake and kicked it on hard, notching it to hold tight. The plunging team of four horses slowed slightly, but not enough. The wild screeching of the brakes seemed, if anything, to add to their frenzy.

Such reins as were still unbroken were out of reach and useless. There was one chance, and only one, to stop the runners before destruction did. Keith lowered himself to the jerking whiffletree, then on to the plunging, swaying tongue of the stagecoach. He made a jump past the heavy hoofs of the wheelers, hands on the backs of each horse for balance.

So far, luck was with him. He had narrowly missed slipping on the tongue, where an error could have sent him off and beneath the flailing hoofs. Now he was at their heads. The trouble was that there was another team in front, and only by controlling the leaders could he manage or control the team as a whole.

Each move now became exceedingly tricky, as did the risk of further frightening the horses, rendering them completely unmanageable. So far they had kept to the road, following it from habit, which was as much luck as training. A wrench on one of the reins beneath a hoof might easily swing them sharply to either side and catastrophe. The threat of a wreck was not past; merely postponed.

Keith balanced on the tip of the twisting, jerking tongue, a task as tricky as that of a spider at the end of a long strand of web, suddenly set swinging in a gale of wind. A miscalculation would be fatal, for while he might escape and roll to the side with no great hurt, the last chance to halt the stage would go with him into the dust of the road.

He launched himself, coming down asprawl on the rump of the right leader, clawing at the harness, dragging himself ahead. The cayuse was quivering under his unusual burden, prevented from wild kicking or bucking only by the racing pull of his teammates.

The road had changed fast, unpleasantly. They were among the hills, with hairpin turns and deep drop-offs at the side. Keith pulled himself forward, holding to the harness, still surprisingly intact. He found a flapping end of an original rein and closed his fingers on it. With his other hand he got hold of the bridle, close up to the mouth.

For the first time he could ease breath back into his lungs, while he pulled strongly on the bit and made his voice even and sure, calling to the team.

It was an ordeal, with the edge of disaster looming first on one side, then on the other. But now he could guide, and the horses responded. Slowly they began to heed him, the wild drum of hoofs pounding less savagely, the rattle of the wheels settling to their usual smooth roll.

They made another mile, a mile in which, had they encountered anyone, disaster must still have resulted. Then the road widened; the drag of the brake was tiring. They eased from gallop to trot, and so to a halt. Blowing, lathered, they looked about distrustfully as Keith slid to the ground.

He used the part of one rein to tie the team to a convenient tree. Then he walked back, and Martha was out of the door and in his arms, trembling, clinging tightly to him as his own arms closed about her.

13.

Despite the runaway pace of the stage during the first part of the day's run, it was well behind its expected schedule when it finally limped into Montana City. Keith was at the reins, with Martha beside him. Repairing the broken harness had been a slow chore; considerable ingenuity had been called for to fashion reins stout enough to control the still uneasy horses. In addition, Keith had turned around and gone back for the driver. As he had feared, he was long past being helped.

No others had come along the road, either to assist or hinder, while those chores were attended to.

The gold camp was going about its usual affairs as though nothing had happened. Keith recognized the signs. Most men were afraid, not only in that camp, but all across the territory of Idaho. At the same time, only a few were frightened enough to run, since to pull up stakes and head out of the country could be even more risky than remaining. Any men who deserted the diggings automatically became an object of suspicion. There was the possibility that he might have made a strike, or that he had been hired to carry gold for some other man.

Indignation might endure for a night, over such callously brutal slayings as had occurred; but with daylight, discretion was the rule. No action on anyone's part could return the dead to life, and it was foolish to go about seeking trouble.

Keith turned the stage, and its late driver, over to the local agent for the company. The latter listened gloomily to the report.

"Another one, eh?" he sighed. "And shot down without no rhyme nor reason—it makes a man wonder!" He surveyed the damaged harness with a sigh. "Thanks for bringin' the stage in. You got passage for Fort Benton?"

"Yes."

"In that case—you wouldn't care to drive it the rest of the way?"

"I'm afraid I wouldn't."

"I figured as much. In that case, as I was sayin', it'll be a while before it's ready to run again. I'll have to find a new driver—and such things happening don't make it no easier."

It was past noon, so they crossed to the usually busy restaurant known as Doug's Beanery. Today, save for a couple of flies which buzzed monotonously, it was empty. A withered little man, his face almost hidden behind an immense crop of hair, appeared in the doorway to the kitchen, surveying them mournfully. He munched disconsolately on a hard dry biscuit and a slice of cold beefsteak. His head shake was regretful.

"I s'pose you're like everybody else—hungry." He sighed. "I'm sorry, but we ain't servin' meals today. We're short a cook, and till I can round up another, there ain't much that I can do about it. I'm no grub-slinger myself. Tried cookin' one time. Emergency to start with, same as now. Made things twice as bad. Liked to lost all the customers I'd had."

"Your regular cook quit?" Keith asked.

"Well, I guess you could call it that, in a manner of speakin'. Chin Yee was too danged efficient for his own good. He could hash up a meal and still have time left over, so when he had some to spare, he liked to go out and muck around in the diggings. Made tobacco money that way. Well, last evenin', while he was doing that, somebody knocked him over the head. From all accounts, it must have been one of them renegades from the gulch. Leastwise, it fits the pattern. Another man was killed a little later—a white man. Armington, his name was. Seems like a man ain't safe anywhere any more. These Vigilantes, they're just stirrin' things up, frightenin' the outlaws to the point where they're out to kill us all."

Keith listened incredulously. Though they had never

met, he had known about Armington and had planned to seek him out and compare notes.

"What makes you think that it was someone from the gulch who did it?" Martha asked.

"Stands to reason," Doug explained. "That's where most of them hang out—Robber's Roost and thereabouts. Likewise, some folks got a look at a newcomer, while he was talkin' to Armington not long before Armington was killed. Recognized him as being from the gulch. Man name of Law."

Martha's face showed strain, but she took this new charge in her stride. The ever-lengthening chain of evidence was too pat, too obviously contrived.

"I'm from the gulch myself," Keith informed the proprietor. "I'll agree with you that there's something mighty unusual going on—and I'd like to find out what it is. Since you're without a cook, would you mind if Martha cooked a meal for the two of us—and for you as well, if you like? There's no other eating place in town, I'm told."

Doug's eyes brightened hopefully.

"You're right about that. Sure, go right ahead, if you're willing. There's a lot of stuff in the kitchen. The Chinee, he liked to have plenty. You're more'n welcome."

He combed fingers through the tangle of whiskers, eying her speculatively.

"Uh—ma'am, while you're about it, would it be

askin' too much for you to maybe sort of cook up enough for some of my reg'lar customers? I promised 'em I'd get somebody by this afternoon, and they've been dependin' on it. It'd be a favor. They've made out poorly today."

"How many are there?" Martha asked.

"Many as you feel like fixin' for. If you could manage somethin' fast but fillin'—"

"I'll see what I can manage," Martha promised, looking around the kitchen approvingly. She lifted the lid of a large kettle, stirred the contents and nodded. "If you'll build a fire in the range, I'll get right at it."

"I'll have a fire in two shakes of a lamb's tail, ma'am —maybe quicker. When folks see smoke, they'll take it as a signal that something's cooking."

Martha was lifting down a neat if oversized apron and tying it on. Her eyes held mute appeal as they fixed on Keith, who was preparing to go out. "Please be careful," she urged.

Keith nodded understandingly. But for her sake as well as his own, this job could not be shirked. He was outraged at the continuing pattern, the evidence which all pointed so relentlessly toward one man. Its very intricacy was a weakness. It was overly obvious, crude.

Or was he allowing his emotions to influence his judgment? John Law was Martha's brother, and to be blinded by his feeling for her could be a fatal mistake. Still worse, such an error would be no kindness to her, if Law was indeed the killer that he was being proclaimed.

Keith could not believe it. With such a sister, it was inconceivable that John Law could do the things of which he stood accused. Equally to the point, Law was no fool. Even granting that he might have gone berserk, he was far too clever to leave such a trail of evidence. Somone was deliberately working to ruin him, to make him appear a monster.

If that premise was accepted, there could be no doubt as to the identity of the other man. Two of the Vigilantes had failed to show up for the meeting back at the gulch. Law was one. The other was McManus.

McManus ducked into a narrow alleyway between two buildings, then stood, fists clenched, until he could control the fit of fury which threatened to undo him. He watched as Keith and Martha picked a course around a mud hole, then went into the restaurant. Surprise, coupled with rage, had almost led to his discovery.

Breathing hard, he accepted the unbelievable. It was like seeing a dead man walking, for Keith should certainly have been dead. What sort of a charmed life did the man lead? Was there no end to his luck?

Somehow, despite the careful plans which McManus had set in motion, Keith was there, obviously unhurt, twice as dangerous.

McManus' own reaction frightened him. Seeing Keith, he had made an involuntary grab for his own gun before realizing the folly of such an action. It would be easy to kill again before Keith even suspected any peril, but the easy way was too dangerous. He must hold onto himself. Killing was becoming a habit, an easy sport which held its own morbid fascination. He was in danger of yielding to impulse, thus wrecking the careful pattern which he had so laboriously contrived.

A few minutes later, he watched Keith emerge from the restaurant, stopping to talk with various men. It was clear by now that Keith was not being fooled by the evidence dangled before his eyes. Probably he had grown suspicious, if not sure of the actual pattern. That was an even stronger reason he had to be disposed of, without loss of time.

But not directly. The lesser risks he could laugh at, but there was Martha to consider. He was directing a campaign against her brother; obviously she had accepted Keith as a friend, a man to be trusted. *Look to the future, man!* he reminded himself. *Some things are beyond a man's explaining.*

A man came along the street, his lopsided appearance due only in part to the heavy gun sagging the holster at his side. McManus called softly.

"Stennis! Keep quiet, man," he went on in a whisper, to forestall an exclamation. "A word with you," he added.

Stennis hesitated, then, recognizing who spoke, ducked into the alleyway alongside the street. Pointedly and concisely, McManus explained what he wanted. Stennis shuffled uneasily as he began to understand.

"Hold on, now," he protested hoarsely. "If you want some killin' done, do it yourself. Why pick on me?"

"Because it has to be done that way," McManus assured him, and held a hand before the other's face. Between thumb and forefinger, he clutched a nugget as big as a dollar. Stennis blinked, then eyed the gold as if mesmerized.

"Do the job, and this is yours," McManus said. "You'll never earn half so much half so easy again."

Stennis gulped, a prominent Adam's apple jiggling in a scrawny throat. Such a nugget was rare and highly desirable.

"I—I don' know," he said huskily. "Folks around here are all stirred up, after what happened last night. It wouldn't take much to start a lynchin' bee—and I ain't cravin' to get stung."

McManus did not argue. He jiggled the nugget in the palm of his hand, then started to return it to a pocket. Stennis' eyes took on a glaze.

"Wait," he implored. "But—why, I ain't even seen the man. I wouldn't know him."

"I'll give you a signal," McManus explained. "There'll be no trouble about that."

Stennis rasped a tongue across eager lips.

"Well—I guess it might be managed. But if they turn on me afterward—"

"They won't. I'll see to that. I'll make folks believe you were a hero."

Stennis regarded him skeptically; then his eyes returned to the nugget. He was torn between avarice and apprehension.

"If you can do that, why don't you do it yourself and get the credit?" he asked doubtfully.

"That's a good question, and I'll tell you," McManus agreed. "I'm a Vigilante, and if I was to be involved in such a way, it would ruin everything."

Stennis' pale eyes widened uneasily. "You're a—not one of them so an' so's—"

"What's so surprising about that?" McManus challenged. "It wasn't easy to work it, but I'm one of that murdering bunch. Do you think we Innocents can last much longer, unless we get them to fighting among themselves and discredit what they are doing? To deal with them, we have to know who they are, all about their plans. That's why I joined them, and why I can't come into the open right now. But Keith is one of them, and he must be stopped now. You ought to be glad to do the job, even without this." Once more, he flashed the nugget before the eyes of Stennis.

The latter nodded. "I guess you're right," he agreed.

14.

Martha swiped sweat from her forehead with the back of a hand and straightened wearily. She had undertaken to prepare a meal upon discovering a large kettle filled with half-cooked stew, which greatly simplified the problem. Nonetheless, since this would be the only meal served today, it had to be a good one for hungry men. She had worked at high speed to make other things ready, also to keep so busily occupied that there would be no time to think. Events had been piling one upon another in nightmarish fashion, and she felt dazed and overwhelmed.

The big coffeepot was boiling, the stew was ready, and she removed two big pans from the oven, filled with biscuits browned to a turn. Their place was taken by two more pans. The word having been passed and the smoke from the chimney observed, the regular customers were filling the outer room to capacity.

"You can pour the coffee and dish up the stew," Martha informed the proprietor. "I'm going to find

Mr. Keith and bring him back, so that we can eat, too."

"Sure, go get him." Doug eyed her hopefully. "Strikes me maybe you're better'n the Chinaman was when it comes to dishin' up tasty grub. You wouldn't consider stayin' on for a while, would you?"

Martha shook her head. "Thanks, but I couldn't," she replied, and went outside. Despite the warmth of the afternoon sun, she was oppressed by a sense of uneasiness. Keith should be returning for the meal. Breakfast at the ranch seemed to be not hours but days ago. If he was half as hungry as she—

Yet hunger was but a small part of what troubled her. If anything should happen to Keith, in addition to what had already occurred—

It was difficult to remember that she had known him less than forty-eight hours. Somehow it seemed much longer, thrown together as they had been by the stress of events. Of one thing she was certain. Her judgment had been sound when she had turned to him. It was believable, right, that she had come to this country to marry him—

A wave of color stained her cheeks and forehead at the truancy of her thoughts. Hastily she looked about. The sun of Indian summer could shine warmly, and today it seemed to come like a benediction upon the camp, as if giving one last benign touch before being shouldered aside by winter. An air of peace, equally misleading, hung over the valley. The mountains were blue in the distance, where the backbone of the country thrust upward.

The camp had an air of desertion. Most men were at work on their claims, the few who indulged in other tasks enjoying a siesta before the busy hours of the evening, when nearly all business was conducted.

She saw Keith coming down the street. He saw her and waved, and Martha thought that his pace accelerated. His eagerness, of course, might be due to hunger and the prospect of satisfying it. Nonetheless, a hint of a smile touched her lips, and she raised a hand instinctively to tuck back a loose lock of hair. She must look a fright—

Her eyes widened, filled suddenly with horror, and a scream tore at her throat. At the same instant a gun lashed savagely against the serenity of the afternoon, and Keith hesitated, wavered, then was floundering in the dust.

Martha ran, her screams still echoing, bringing the barely seated restaurant customers off their stools and out of doors, rousing other life along the somnolent road as the gunshot alone could not have done. The roar of exploding gunpowder was a fairly common occurrence, but the desperate scream of a woman was rare.

She reached Keith and dropped on her knees beside him, then cradled his bloody head in her lap. To her anguished relief, his eyes opened, dazed and filled with pain, then clearing somewhat as they rested on her face. He shook his head in bewilderment, grimacing afresh at the movement.

"What happened?"

"You were shot," she explained, then looked up fiercely as the others began to crowd around. "I saw it all!" she cried. "There was a tall, slouching man with a gun—he was wearing a blue and white checkered shirt. And McManus was standing not far away. He signaled the man to shoot. I saw that, too!"

She explained in more detail as excited questions were asked, and some of the men set off, running, grim-faced. With her assistance, Keith got to his feet. He was shaky, but decided that he was not greatly hurt, aside from the blood along his scalp, and an aching head.

The wound was slight, though another inch to the side would have been fatal. His skull had been creased by the bullet, which had momentarily knocked him out but had stopped just short of being serious. Martha's scream, coming at the instant when Stennis had squeezed the trigger, had startled the outlaw, partially spoiling his aim.

In the next few minutes, as men compared notes and listened anew to her description of the gunman, it was agreed that it must have been Stennis.

"Ain't nothing very surprising about that," one of the bystanders observed. "He's a no-good sort who's been hangin' around lately, never seeming to have nothing to do. But are you sure about McManus, and him givin' Stennis a signal? Why, I was talkin' to McManus not an hour ago. You must have misunderstood what he was doing, or something."

"I wasn't mistaken," Martha assured them. "As it happens, I've known Mr. McManus for quite a while, though I hadn't seen him for a long time. But I know of my own experience that he is a scoundrel, and I saw his signal very clearly. He lifted an arm, then pointed unmistakably at Mr. Keith as he came along. What McManus was doing attracted my attention, and I looked to see whom he was signaling.

"The gunman—Stennis—was partly hidden in that little opening between those two buildings. He was watching McManus, and when the signal was given, he nodded and raised his gun. When I saw where he was aiming, I screamed."

"Sounds convincin' enough, the way you tell it," the other man acknowledged. "And one sure thing bears you out: neither of them lost any time makin' themselves scarce. Though you can't rightly blame them, under the circumstances."

"I don't think there's the slightest question that McManus is guilty," Keith observed, "not only of pointing me out to Stennis, but also of those killings in town last night. I can understand why this may surprise some of you, for I had courted him as a friend up to a day or so ago. But after what's been happening—"

He went on to explain the chain of circumstances, starting at Pine Grove. He omitted any reference to the Vigilantes, and the membership of Law, McManus and himself in the organization.

"Burden was my friend, too," he explained. "So I set out to try and discover who had killed him in such a fashion. It boiled down to one of two men—John Law or McManus. Both of them had left the gulch in a hurry, under suspicious circumstances.

"For a while, I was pretty sure that Law was the guilty man, and the evidence has kept piling up— along with his apparently being seen here in the camp last evening. But that trail of evidence adds up to too much of the same thing. If he was guilty, he'd never leave so open a trail. Also, I went and had a look at the place where Armington was killed last night."

The others were listening respectfully, grim and tense. The indisputable fact that Stennis had tried to murder Keith lent weight to what he had to say. The further evidence of a beautiful woman that McManus had given Stennis the signal was not lightly to be passed over.

"As I've told you, I knew both Law and McManus well—and counted both of them as friends. I'm told that last night the killer was seen wearing Law's clothes, which is entirely possible. McManus is about of a build with him, and could have gotten hold of a coat and hat. Where they differ is in the size of their feet. McManus has a big foot. He wears a boot at least three sizes bigger than Law's. I once heard him joke about the difference.

"Where Armington was killed, I found two sets of boot prints in the dirt—and one, I made sure, belonged to Armington. He had a pattern of hobnails that can't be mistaken. The sign is still there for anybody who wants to take a look. The other set must have belonged to his killer—and he had big feet!"

"There's something more, which pretty well clinches it." Another man, panting, had come up in time to hear the last part. "I've been chasin' McManus, but he got on a horse and got away. Being afoot, with no horse handy, I couldn't follow. But he was in a mighty big hurry, and as he was scramblin' into the saddle, he dropped something. Here it is."

He held up a coat, which Keith had no difficulty in identifying. It had belonged to Law.

"That seems to settle it, then. He must have been wearin' that last night. So it's McManus we need to get—not Law."

There was no argument, but neither was there pursuit. Most men were too occupied with their own work to take off upon a probably hopeless chase, and what had happened was not new. The word would spread, and McManus woud be a marked, though not necessarily a hunted man. The Innocents were numerous and, as everybody knew, well organized. More than one known highwayman or killer swaggered openly through the streets of the camps, daring anyone to lift a hand against him.

Oblique, considering glances were cast at Keith. He spoke with more knowledge and conviction than most, in itself a matter for speculation. It might be that the Vigilantes would do something about the reign of terror. A start had been made, which so far had induced a savage reaction. Men suddenly remembered the dinner which they had barely tasted, or other tasks, and hurried off to see about them.

Holding Keith's arm, Martha guided him back to the kitchen. Though a bit wobby on his legs, Keith could have managed by himself, but it was pleasant to have her so solicitous.

The second batch of biscuits came hot from the oven. They said little as they ate, but a new bond of understanding was forged between them, the weight of an uneasy sense of guilt removed where her brother was concerned. The virtual certainty that Law was not his quarry made Keith feel light-headed.

After Martha had declined anew the offer to cook for the restaurant, they went outside again. Keith was feeling the effects of the bullet which had grazed his scalp, though it was a reminder that it could easily have been worse.

"That was a point-blank shot, and he'd have killed

me, sure, if you hadn't distracted him as you did," he observed.

"I thought he was going to," Martha agreed, and her fingers tightened convulsively on his arm. "It was horrible."

"You said that you used to know McManus," Keith reminded her. "Mind telling me about it?"

"It was back east, more than a year ago. The—it's rather difficult to explain—" She colored, then went on gravely.

"He fell in love with me. At least that's what he called it. Actually, as I know now, I was only a means to an end, as is the case with everything he does. One obstacle in his way was that he wasn't in a very good position to press his suit. He had been in trouble with the army, and was more or less on the run."

Keith nodded. "The pattern hasn't changed."

"I'm afraid it never does with such a man. From what I've been able to learn, I suspect that he was actually a double agent, in both the Union and the Confederate armies, and a traitor to each side whenever it suited his purpose. He always worked for himself. One result was that it became safer for him to head west."

"A lot of folks go west for such reasons of health."

"McManus is a very able man, in his way, and completely unscrupulous. I won't bother you with a lot of details, but many things which I once found hard to believe I now know to be so. I know that he has worked to bring about a situation so difficult for my brother and me that, to extricate ourselves, I would be compelled to marry him. Not that his chief interest is in me. We have property which he covets, and hopes to obtain in that fashion."

"It fits the pattern."

"Just how he managed certain matters, I don't know, but there was false testimony involving my brother, connecting him with treasonable activities. The chance that John headed west at just about that time played ino McManus' hands, making it appear as if he were fleeing. Apparent flight seemed to amount to a confession of guilt.

"I knew by then that it was all a monstrous plot, and I had some friends who helped. Through them, I managed to find evidence which would refute McManus' accusations. Armed with that, I came west to try and find John and give him the information before it was too late."

"How do you mean?"

"McManus had some influential friends, and proceedings have been instituted, including a court hearing, with a time limit. Unless John appears to defend himself—and I'm sure that he doesn't even know about any of this—then he will automatically be adjudged guilty. Should he return east after that, he would face a long prison sentence. But the real crux of the whole plot is that, if he is found guilty of treasonable activities, our property is forfeit. Exactly how McManus intends to get much of it in such an event I don't know, but I'm sure he has it all worked out with officials as unscrupulous as himself. He is playing for big stakes, and he has boasted that I'll see the light and marry him, as the only way to clear the family name and to regain a share of what is already ours."

Keith pondered. Knowing McManus, he was convinced it was entirely credible. Here was no two-bit, tinhorn gambler, but a man with ability to match his imagination. It was no wonder that McManus had become a power among The Innocents, or that he had also managed to penetrate the Vigilante organization. Keith had seen plenty of evidence of his genius for leadership.

Certainly he would not stop now. There was too much at stake, including his life.

A driver had been found, and the stage was ready to roll again. Keith surveyed Martha anxiously.

"Are you too tired to go on?" he asked. "It may get rougher before it gets better."

"Do we have any choice?" she asked, and to that there was only one answer. There could be no pause, no let-down.

15.

McManus was first of all a realist. He could plan big and execute with a broad sweep, and he always made allowances for setbacks. Handicaps which would ruin a lesser man he generally managed to turn to good account. It had been necessary to head west, to a land beyond the reach of law, while the caldron which he had so vigorously stirred cooled somewhat.

By now it should be safe to return, under another name and guise, to complete plans already begun. Meanwhile, he had done very well for himself along the frontier.

His problem for the moment was Keith. The man was a stumbling block, and threatened to become a menace. McManus knew that he was in no immediate danger; still, the long-range risk had been increased. Forced to flee in uncalculated fashion, he had looked back to see Keith getting to his feet, apparently not much hurt. A heartfelt cursing of Stennis, and others who had blundered, scarcely relieved his feelings. The damage was done, and Keith's luck still held.

Worse, Keith and Martha would spread the word, making him a fugitive, and after the wanton killings at the camp, it would be prudent to put a lot of distance between Montana City and himself. He was used to such a role, and since he was about to leave the country in any case, it didn't greatly matter. He could even find certain virtues in flight. Keith and Martha would inevitably follow, and even the longest run of luck would have to end. He'd see that it did in Keith's case, and take pleasure in the doing.

His mistake had lain in entrusting the job to others, men who by nature were bunglers. The worst of it was that he had not even profited by such indirect dealing. The careful chain of evidence which he had built up against Law had been ruined, at least in that neighborhood, and his own position undermined.

McManus sighed. He'd preferred the indirect approach, since Martha was involved. But it was clear that he had to make sure by doing things himself.

He hadn't noticed the loss of the coat, Law's coat, until it had worked loose from the saddle and fallen as he was taking off. It would be evidence against him, though that didn't matter too much. There were ways of handling almost any situation.

The part which bothered him most was that Keith would continue to travel with Martha. Events which he had sought to raise as a barrier between were only fencing them together. The thought was like a poisoned barb. More than ever, he was determined Keith must die.

John Law must be somewhere ahead, but he probably wouldn't know that the situation had changed. He'd still suppose that he was a hunted man. . . .

This was a country of hills. They were sub-ranges, offshoots of the great divide, with an annoying habit of thrusting themselves up in unexpected places, necessitating weary climbs to traverse them. McManus had little interest in hills and even less in the names given them, berating them impartially. One more divide was in the way, and after that the land fell away in long gradual slopes toward the river called the Sun, and the town of the same name. Beyond that again, a considerable distance beyond, was the big river, the Missouri, and old Fort Benton. It could be termed old only by comparison with the upstart camps at Bannack and those clustered along the golden gulch.

Antelope materialized out of a meadow and flashed away with a show of white flags. McManus' cayuse snorted and sought to emulate them in a display of fright and speed. It whirled, plunging, and loose gravel slid under its hoofs. Scrambling frantically, it slid a score of feet below the road, then brought up, trembling and really dismayed. The consternation spread to McManus as he saw that its mock show of terror had lamed it.

The horse limped badly, and neither the spur nor the quirt made any appreciable difference. Apparently a tendon had been strained, and for the next several days, the horse would be virtually useless.

McManus skirted the rim of panic. This was thinly settled country, and the miles stretched formidably. The knowledge that he was a hunted man was not reassuring.

Smoke made a wispy question mark above the leafless tops of cottonwoods. It came from a quarter of a mile beyond the road, up a narrow, canyon-like valley, with hills rising steeply at either side. From the road, only the smoke was visible, but there was a wheel trace, fairly fresh. There might be a cabin back in there, and beggars could not be choosers. Dismounting, McManus led his horse; its limp increased.

With luck, he might be able to make a trade. All that was required was to find a good animal. He carried the luck in his holster.

The worst part was walking for any distance. However pleasant the awareness that his money belt bulged with gold, it was burdensome since his double strike at Montana City. It would be a relief when he could rid himself of it.

A cluster of buildings appeared, filling a tiny meadow near the head of the gulch. All had a look of newness, some not yet complete, but all bearing the imprint of untiring industry. McManus frowned, perplexed. He had expected nothing like this. Even for a ranch, this was ambitious in scope, and the site, hidden among the hills, seemed to indicate a recluse or perhaps a crackpot. It had been his observation that, despite its scantiness of population, the frontier had its full share of the latter.

That made no difference, if he could obtain what he wanted, and the size of the operation was reassuring. McManus went on, pausing an instant in dismayed understanding. A man crossed from one building to another, and the fleeting impression was like that of a woman.

A part of the mystery was explained. The man was a black robe— friar, brother or priest, McManus was uncertain as to the proper designation. In any case, it did not matter. He recalled having heard of a mission being set up somewhere among these hills, apparently to preach to the Indians. This must be it, and it should do well enough for his purpose.

He walked on, his hesitation scarcely noticeable. It was unlikely that these withdrawn, simple-minded men would have heard of him. There should be no difficulty.

Another man appeared as he neared the buildings. He too was black-robed, his round face gravely solemn. McManus doffed his hat politely.

"This is my lucky day, Father, to find such a place," he observed. "My horse has gone lame—the poor beast."

Its condition was obvious. The other man's face showed concern.

"The poor beast is indeed lame," he conceded, running a hand along the injured leg. "There is a stall in the barn, and hay. If you will care for it, then come on to the house; we will make you welcome to such as we have. Now I beg that you will excuse me, as we are somewhat disrupted at the moment and very busy."

"Think nothing of it, Father," McManus assured him. "I am used to doing for myself."

The friar nodded absently and disappeared. McManus stabled his horse, observing with disappointment that the barn was empty of other animals. But at least it was a secluded place, and few who passed along the road would be likely to notice it, unless they chanced to see smoke, as he had done.

He crossed to the house, encountering another man who wore no robe. He appeared to be a workman. McManus was relieved. Religion, of late, had been rather outside his experience.

"Is it a mission you build here?" he asked.

"So it is." The reply was somewhat disconcerting. "The cattle on a thousand hills—"

The quotation was left hanging in the air, while the other man regarded him expectantly. McManus coughed.

"Er—quite so. I was wondering—I have an excellent horse, but it has gone lame, and I am in somewhat of a hurry. Might it be possible to make a trade for another animal—in exchange for whatever compensation may be fair?"

"Brother Sebastian makes all such decisions. Unfortunately, Brother Sebastian is too ill to be bothered with any sort of problem at the moment."

"I'm sorry to hear that. But I'd make the trade worth your while—"

"Right now, there's not another horse on the place. Brother Jonas has the team; he is bringing supplies from Sun River. We anticipate his arrival sometime tomorrow. Brother Felix accompanied him, riding our only saddle horse. So until they return—" Again he eyed McManus expectantly.

McManus strove to hide his dismay. If there was no horse of any sort, he'd simply have to wait until one was available. It was out of the question to proceed on foot, burdened as he was. He clutched at a remembered fragment out of his youth.

"The Lord's will be done," he murmured piously.

Apparently it was the right answer. The other man led the way inside.

"I suppose the Brothers can put you up, at least for the night," he observed somewhat doubtfully. "Things won't be fancy, you understand."

"I wouldn't expect anything of the sort," McManus protested.

"If you did, this would not be the place to find it.

Simplicity is the keynote." He went out, as the first man whom McManus had encountered entered, shaking his head.

"You are welcome to such simple hospitality as we can offer," he said. "But you come upon us at a trying moment. Brother Sebastian—I fear that he is dying."

"Dying? The poor man!" McManus was properly sympathetic. "What a time for me to intrude! On the other hand," he went on, with sudden inspiration, "possibly I can be of help. I am not without skill along such lines. Once I planned to become a physician, and gave considerable study to the art."

He was regarded with new interest, even a gleam of hope. "Your arrival may be providential, an answer to prayer. If you will have a look at him, then—"

Brother Sebastian lay stretched on an austerely simple cot, a gaunt man of advanced years. It required no more than a look to confirm the already expressed opinion that he was very sick. He neither opened his eyes nor gave any sign of awareness as McManus felt his pulse, which was a bare flutter. Two others in black robes were kneeling in prayer on either side of the bed. McManus clucked his tongue sympathetically and shook his head.

"The poor man." He sighed. "It is too late for the things of this earth. Already, I fear, his soul wings its way to heaven."

From another room came the noise of hammering

and sawing, punctuated by a crash. As they withdrew, the first brother winced.

"Poor Mike," he sighed. "He tries hard, but without Brother Sebastian's direction, he is like a small boy, playing with the tools of men. He seeks to put together a coffin," he added. "For all of us, it becomes a thing of vexation."

"Why then, perhaps I can help," McManus suggested. "I have an affinity for saw and hammer and the slicing of boards. Allow me to assist, since for the other I was not in time."

"If you can make it fit properly, so it will be a decent resting place for our good Brother, you will earn our gratitude," he was assured. The workman straightened at their approach, mopping his face, eying his handiwork ruefully.

"When Brother Sebastian directs, or saws the boards, everything goes well." He sighed. "But somehow, though I measure before I cut, the boards seem never to come out as intended."

"That is soon corrected," McManus assured him, and was as good as his word. Bidding the harassed assistant to see to his other neglected duties, he proceeded to put the box together, doing a workmanlike job. Hushed voices came to his ears, making it clear that Brother Sebastian had indeed departed this earth and so needed a final resting place.

Since he had to tarry awhile there, it would be well

to earn the gratitude of his hosts, against possible eventualities.

He was putting the finishing touches to the box, noting that the declining sun was already gone from sight in the narrow embrasure of this canyon-like valley, when he caught a fresh sound. Whether welcome or not he was far from certain, since it was made by several horses, pulling up outside. A little later their riders came trampling and jingling into the house.

McManus hesitated, then continued working, keeping at an even tempo, while contriving to listen to what was said. There were horses in the yard, and a horse was what he needed. There were four good cayuses, as he could glimpse from a small window.

The difficulty was that the men who had ridden them there were Vigilantes, and they were looking for him.

16.

So far, no one appeared to have any suspicion that the man they sought might be anywhere in the vicinity, certainly not that he might be sheltered in the mission. The conversation was along general lines, which did not seem to carry any particular meaning to the other-worldly minds of the brothers.

The posse — for unmistakably that was what it amounted to—had turned in there, hoping to get some supper. Since hospitality was the rule, they were being courteously received, despite the difficult situation. What had happened was explained to them, and like McManus, they were properly sympathetic.

"If we'd known about that, of course we wouldn't have intruded on you folks—"

"You did not know, and your coming is not an intrusion. Do we not ask that our daily bread be given? And when a loaf is asked of us, shall we respond with a stone? Such fare as we have is yours to share, and welcome."

McManus glanced uneasily at the lengthening shadows outside. Perhaps he could chance a try, helping him to a horse before anyone noticed, then driving the other cayuses ahead of him, to guard against pursuit.

For the moment such a course would be highly risky, but to remain was equally so. He poised a hand above his gun, then went on working as he saw that it was one of the black robes who had entered the room.

"We are about to break our fast," he explained, "along with our other guests. Will you not join us?"

McManus shook his head. "I am grateful, not to say hungry," he returned. "But this task is almost done. I would prefer to put the finishing touches to it while the light holds. Once it is done, I can eat with better relish."

"You are doing a workmanlike job. Also, as you say, the light fades. Unfortunately, we have no candles with which to light the room. But you place us in your debt."

Never, in a varied career, had McManus spent so unusual or tense an evening. It had grown reasonably dark outside, so gloomy inside that he could barely complete his puttering, which by now was unnecessary save as an excuse. But when he glanced outside again, it was to see a red eye winking back, like the baleful gze of Moloch.

McManus stiffened, muttering words scarcely befitting the edifice. One of the men had finished his supper, then had gone outside to enjoy a cigar. As long as he lounged by the horses, it was risky to try to get one.

Thoughtfully, grateful for what McManus had done, one of the brothers brought him a tray.

"It occurred to me that you might prefer to eat here," he said. "I take it that you are a simple man, ill at ease in the rough presence of many who abide in this wild land."

"Indeed, you are thoughtful, and such men do fill me with a kind of terror," McManus agreed fervently. "As you say, I am an ordinary person, one who inclines to be alone. The life which you lead here has much to commend it."

The immediate crisis was past, but the red eye still winked from the gloom outside. McManus ate his supper, drinking the water which accompanied it with wry distaste, relieved when the other visitors finally went outside. But then they lost no time before riding away, and his chance to acquire a horse was gone.

Resignedly he accepted a cot in a small room, thankful for the chance to lie down. There was nothing else to do, unless he abandoned his laden money-belt, and that was unthinkable.

It was still a long two-day journey, with a good horse, to Fort Benton. So a horse he must have.

Sleep brought refreshment, but morning brought new problems. The others had composed Brother Sebastian for his last rest, laying him out in the coffin. It must now be closed, the half-door fitted and fastened in place. Their chief worry was how they would get it to the cemetery. Unlike most boot hills in that careless land, their plot of ground was located a couple of miles from the mission, farther along the road. The grave, they explained, had been prepared, but there was still no sign of Brother Jonas with the horses and wagon. Yet it seemed best that their brother should be interred without undue delay.

"I will close the coffin," McManus offered, once breakfast had been eaten. "That is the least that I can do to repay you for your hospitality."

Since his workmanship with wood was superior to what the others could manage, they accepted gratefully. Certain rites, which McManus watched in what passed for a respectful silence, were completed; then they repaired to another room for some sort of a service, leaving him to finish his task. Brother Sebastian wore a peaceful look.

The door required a bit of work to make it fit smoothly. He was putting the finishing touches to that when a fresh clatter of hoofs sounded from outside.

The sun was high enough to penetrate into the steep-walled valley, and to catch and slide along the stuffed chambers of guns protruding from holsters. The quartette of the previous evening were back, and something in the way they rode was a warning. McManus looked about uneasily. There was no place to hide, no chance to flee.

He hesitated, fingering his own gun. Should he start shooting the instant anyone appeared at the door, he could probably get a couple of them. That would not be good enough, for some of the four would certainly get him in turn.

He toyed momentarily with a philosophic notion. This might be a fitting place in which to die, inside a mission house, beside a man who had dedicated his life to the service of his fellow-man. The chance of dying in so rarefied an atmosphere was not likely to come again.

The trouble was that he had no desire to be cast, even remotely, in the role of a martyr. To be trapped in any case verged on outrage. It had been a matter of a single day since everything had been going as he liked—

McManus moved fast. Sounds indicated that the man-hunters were interrupting the service being conducted in another room, somewhat apologetic as they understood, but none the less determined and in a hurry. One ran to the barn, returning almost at once to report:

"It's his horse, all right. It's gone lame. So he can't be far off."

Distressed by these developments, which they comprehended only in part, the brothers were confirming that the owner of the horse was indeed a guest of the house. He was a mild, unassuming, almost dedicated man; it could not be that the others actually sought him as an outlaw. There must be some mistake.

"There's no mistake," one of the newcomers assured them, the sound carrying clearly. "He's McManus, from the gulch—and he killed a couple of men at Montana City a couple of nights ago. It was cold-blooded murder. We picked up what looked like a clue this morning and headed back this way. If we'd only guessed, last night—"

That far the talk went, and then they burst into the room, guns drawn, but not rashly. Two came by way of the door, their companions by way of the window, gun snouts thrusting ahead. It promised to be not only a disagreeable chore but a dangerous one, but they were not in a mood to shirk. McManus was far too big a menace to leave at large.

Inside, they hesitated, at a loss. The window stood partly open, but not wide enough for a man to crawl through. The coffin sat on a pair of sawhorses, and the room was pungent with the odor of sawdust and fresh shavings. Carpenter's tools were ranged on hooks and a shelf. Otherwise the room was empty.

Baffled, they spread out in a hasty search. It seemed that he must have gotten through the window, but they were not convinced of that, especially when it stuck, refusing to open wider. They prowled like hungry hounds, an elusive whiff of scent tickling their nostrils, finding the trail too tangled to follow.

McManus lay stretched in the coffin, holding his breath and his gun, with the lid fitted neatly into place above him. Close inspection might have revealed that it had not been fastened shut. Angrily he berated himself for a foolish move.

The loose squeak of one of the rough-hewn floor boards had first intrigued his curiosity as he worked. It had come loose at a tug, and he had been of a mind to nail it solidly in place. Instead he had left it, seeing that beneath there was just room enough for a man to lie outstretched. Having taken due note of that, he had replaced the board.

What he should have done was to fit himself into that space beneath the floor. Instead, hurried and on the verge of panic, he had lifted out Brother Sebastian and dumped him unceremoniously down there, then had taken his place in the coffin. On second thought it was not the best choice, but it was too late to change.

Apparently the Brothers, like the posse, assumed that he had escaped through the window. Troubled and disturbed by recent events, they strove to remain calm, not to seem lacking in hospitality, even to scarcely welcome guests.

Except for stirrings and more distant sounds, a troubled calm had succeeded the flurry. McManus was puzzled as to what they were about, then decided that a couple of them must be kneeling in prayer on either side of the coffin.

A pair of horsemen rode away, but other sounds indicated that a couple of the Vigilantes were remaining, convinced that he was hiding in the vicinity. McManus strove to compose himself.

Sure and I'm laid out for burying, he reminded himself grimly. And those words would be a fitting epitaph, were they meant for me—which they are not! One of the Brothers was now praying audibly. Well, they haven't tossed dirt in my face—not yet!

Resigning himself to patience was far from easy. He had lingered there much longer than he'd intended; something always seemed to interfere at crucial moments. But perhaps the quartette would soon tire of the hunt and go away. He would like nothing better than to do the same.

His trouble now was threefold. He still lacked a horse, the possession of which had become imperative. Aside from the Vigilantes, the Brothers also would be hostile. They might not lift a hand to stop him, but they would surely be unfriendly, horrified at the manner in which he had abused their hospitality, enraged should they discover his manner of dealing with Brother Sebastian.

The thought brought a grim smile to his face. Brother Sebastian had nothing of which to complain.

His troubles were over. McManus had seen graves which the wolves and Indians had desecrated. A safe haven under a floor was certainly better.

A measure of peace seemed to have returned. He wondered if he dared risk pushing up the lid enough for a look, and a breath of fresh air. Inside, it was both hot and cramped and increasingly stuffy. But a wrong move could be fatal.

Desperate, he risked it, lifting the lid a bit at a time, striving to see out. There was no view possible from so restricted a position, and someone was returning. He lowered the door again.

To his surprise, the box was lifted, carried laboriously out through a door, lifted higher, and set, not too gently, into place. There were voices, and words which he could not quite catch. Then he was moving, jolted uncomfortably. The wagon must have returned, and the coffin was being taken on it out to the road toward the cemetery.

McManus shivered, fighting a sense of panic. They had a couple of miles to go, but that wouldn't take very long. After the place was reached, he supposed there would be a final ritual or service before the grave was filled in. It was up to him to get out before the destination was attained; otherwise so many would be gathered that a nasty mess would result.

Surprise, a shock horrifying to the others, would be in his favor when the lid was raised up and the corpse crawled from the coffin. By making full use of that moment, he could probably make good his escape, at least if he used his gun.

To his surprise, McManus found himself shrinking from that possibility. It was bad enough already for these poor devils of Brothers, without killing some of them—

He had killed men many times without compunction, giving no more thought to the matter than if the victim were a bobcat or coyote. His justification, when he had considered it at all, had been that they would do the same to him if given the chance. But so cynical a philosophy did not apply to these wearers of the black robes. The trouble was that they were just not fitted to cope with life or death on the frontier.

Judging by the sounds of wheels and hoofs, the grassy side-trail into the little valley had been traversed, and they were back on the hard-packed main road which led on toward Sun River. It wound and climbed toward the crest of the divide. Apparently they had chosen a resting place high up, near to the heaven they sought.

He could distinguish nothing except the sound of the wagon wheels and the fainter clop of hoofs. Probably the Brothers were marching in a group somewhere behind, or they might have gone ahead. They could even be taking a short cut instead of following the road. At any rate, it was now or never. And it had not been in his plan, when working at it, to fashion this coffin for himself.

McManus tossed back the cover and sat up, gulping a breath of fresh air. Never had it seemed sweeter. He would be more than happy to depart in peace, to steal away unobserved—

It was not to be. At the sound, the driver swiveled on the seat to look, and his eyes bulged. His face, ruddy as a scarlet berry, took on a mottled hue, and his jaw sagged. Abruptly, with a frantic yell and in a single jump, he was off the wagon and running. McManus watched appreciatively.

Should anything as slow as a jack rabbit chance to get in his way, it would simply be outclassed and kicked aside.

17.

McManus sighed. He had little time to waste, even on such an exhibition of footwork. The Brothers who accompanied the makeshift hearse would be ahead or behind, but they were temporarily hidden from view, and the opportunity was too good to waste.

He surveyed the wagon, debating whether to whip up the horses and attempt escape in it. But it was heavily loaded, and the road ahead was growing steeper.

It struck him as odd that it should be so heavily laden, even without the casket. Goods of various kinds had been packed in the double box, then covered with a stained and torn tarp. The coffin had been set atop all the rest and tied in place with a rope. It seemed strange that they had not first unloaded the supplies back at the mission.

Since they had not, the wagon would be a hindrance instead of a help. He preferred something faster and less conspicuous, as well as more maneuverable; preferably a horse, which could leave the road behind.

The team had come to a prompt stop as the driver dropped the reins and fled. The animals were built for pulling, not the saddle, and long effort had worn them down, so that their only interest was to stop at every opportunity. Even the driver's terror had not stirred them from their apathy.

McManus came clear of his cramped coach and down to the road. An instant later he was out of sight among the brush at the side. He gave no second thought to the disruption he caused to the funeral arrangements or to the possibility that never again might he have a chance for so fine a burial, among so select a company of mourners.

As a boy, Law had reveled in games of hide and seek, savoring the excitement of the chase. Being a participant in reality was certainly as exciting, but there the parallel ended. He would thankfully have yielded his place in what had become no game but a desperate fight for existence.

The difficulty lay in extricating himself from the situation. He was a hunted man, fair game alike for the law-abiding or the outlaws who so mockingly called themselves The Innocents. Being hunted was bad enough. The necessity for haste rendered matters worse.

The need for speed came from the belated receipt of a letter from his sister. In it, she had informed him somewhat disjointedly of events in the East; also that she was making her way to Idaho Territory as quickly as possible, to find and join him. There were too many questions to which he had no answers for his peace of mind, but it seemed likely that she might even now be in the country, perhaps at Fort Benton. Thus haste in reaching her became imperative.

For the last several hours the hide and seek part had been particularly grim. He'd taken the caution of skirting widely around Montana City, temporarily leaving the hills and chancing the more flat open country, where a man on a horse would be visible for long distances—especially on a pinto pony.

That hazard lay behind him, but though he was once more among the mountains, trouble had been on the prowl. Law had been placed in the ambiguous position of recognizing a quartette of riders who had been his friends and might be again, if proper communication and understanding could be reestablished. Lacking that vital link, he deemed it better to go his separate way.

The problem was that they had sighted him, recognizing at least the pinto, and seemed determined to hunt him down. He had been compelled to waste time playing the game, hiding, circling, resorting to every trick or artifice of which he was capable. That he had not done too badly was attested by his continuing freedom of choice and action.

The hunt had continued well into the night, the searchers aided by a reasonable display of moon and stars. When at length heavy blackness had rendered the hunt impractical, it had been too late for him to keep going. Law and his horse had been on the verge of exhaustion.

Morning brought a bit of luck. He'd managed a single meal the day before, not being able to adapt himself as did his horse and eat grass at every pause. Awakening, he discovered a sage hen blinking at him from only a few feet away. Such birds were notoriously stupid and slow to take alarm, a trait which had been the salvation of many a hungry man.

It gave promise of being the case now. Law's fingers closed on a stone. He lifted his arm, then threw. His aim proved good. The land lay wide and empty, or at least it gave that illusion in the brightening dawn. Law gathered dry sticks and built a small, nearly smokeless fire deep in a small coulee, then set about roasting the fowl.

The trouble with such wood was that it consumed swiftly, giving scant heat. He was at the coulee's crest, having foraged for additional fuel, when a shot sounded from close at hand. Not that it had noise or meaning in Law's ears. By the time it reached him, the bullet loosed by the blast of powder had outrun it, and he was pitching into oblivion, rolling and tumbling down a slope toward the road below.

This particular run of the Bannack stage to Benton
seemed plagued by ill luck. In the golden gulch there
had been delay, caused by difficulties stemming from
the preceding run; at Three Forks, fresh trouble had
hindered them; then the killing of the driver and the
near-wrecking of the stage had made things even
worse.

On leaving Montana City, they had not gone far
when a wheel, in worse condition than anyone had
supposed, had broken as it bumped over a big stone
embedded in the road.

Fortunately, as had been the case at Illman's, another
ranch lay only a mile or so at the side, and they were
able to spend the night there and, still better, to obtain
a replacement wheel. Philosophical by nature, the new
driver estimated that they were running almost on
schedule as they took off again the next morning.

"Just one day late," he said. "And what's a day,
when it's gone?"

Apparently delays were not at an end. They topped
an easy slope, to find a strange spectacle blocking the
road. A laden freight wagon was surrounded by several
men in black robes, men who seemed to be suspended
on both horns of a dilemma. Anger, which they strove
to control as unseemly, and mystification and distress
had left them bewildered and uncertain.

Keith discovered that he had a personal interest in
what was happening there. The wagon was his own—

the one he had dispatched from the gulch some days before, with a driver and cargo bound for Benton.

There was no sign of the driver, which puzzled the Brothers as much as it did him. They had been out of sight of the impromptu hearse for only a short while. Everything had seemed to be normal. Then they had heared a wild yell and, coming in sight, had found the wagon deserted, the team standing, thankful for the chance to rest. That was unusual enough, but it was only the beginning.

The lid of the coffin had been removed. Now the coffin was revealed to be empty of the body of Brother Sebastian.

Contrary to the assumption of McManus when the coffin had been loaded, it had not been placed on the supply wagon, because that had not returned from Sun River. Since the movements of the wagon on such a journey were uncertain, they had hailed the freight wagon as it came along the road, explaining their dilemma and requesting a favor. Would the driver be so obliging as to render service unto God and man alike by allowing them to load the coffin atop his other cargo? It would not be out of his way to take it as far as the hilltop cemetery farther along the road.

It had been an unusual request, and it was surprising to come upon black-robed friars in that out-of-the way place, where he had not even suspected their existence. Having had recourse to a bottle at intervals along the way to fortify himself against the rigors of the road, the driver had been unsure as to how much was reality and how much might be illusion. Men who wore skirts like women were outside his experience and to be viewed with suspicion. To a mind already befuddled by alcohol, the whole thing bordered on the fantastic.

Nonetheless, he had been willing to oblige. He had driven off the road and up the canyon to the mission, still not entirely convinced about it. The box had been loaded on and tied in place, and he had returned to the road, resuming the journey toward a spot which one of the Brothers piously referred to as God's Acre. Never had he heard of such a place, but the sound was somehow unchancy.

Like the garb and manner of the Brothers, each new development served further to confuse him. He had fortified himself with another quick pull at the bottle, convinced that what was happening was all the figment of a dream. There was really no coffin riding behind him, with all that such a thing implied—

A sound caused him to turn in time to discover the dead in the process of what he could only regard as an untimely resurrection. Out from the abode of the dead was one who rose up and looked at him. That had been enough and too much. He had taken off, and he had no intention of returning.

Enough of this was conveyed for Keith to understand what must have happened. The coffin was empty, the driver gone. One of the Brothers sought, by explaining recent events, to shed light upon the strange events, a clarification also needed by his own groping mind.

"I fear that we are unworldly, ill fitted to cope with the problems of so harried an existence," he confessed. "Our purpose, in establishing this mission here on the frontier, was twofold—not only to minister to our red brothers of the plains, but also to found a retreat, a solace apart from the workaday world. Brother Sebastian alone was trained to deal with such problems as might arise. And now that he is gone—"

His glance alighted on the empty coffin, and he wrung his hands, clutching convulsively within the folds of his robe.

"Gone, but where? What could have caused the material body of our good Brother to vanish, and the driver of the wagon to take flight in such fashion?"

"It looks as though whoever was occupying the coffin must have climbed out of it," Keith hazarded. "Which could be reason enough for the driver to go somewhere else in a hurry!"

"But such a thing is impossible! How could he, as you put it, climb out? Brother Sebastian—may the saints have him in their keeping!—was unmistakably dead. He must have been. Yet I am bewildered. There has been so much excitement and confusion that I can no longer think coherently. Even since that rogue McManus arrived, a wolf in the guise of a lost sheep—"

"McManus?" Keith ejaculated. "I think that I begin to understand. Tell me about him."

Gradually he elicited the story from them: how helpful the newcomer had been, how dismayed they had felt when the man-hunters had come and made plain that their guest was a fugitive, with black crimes charged against him. The tale had been difficult to believe of so kindly and helpful a man; moreover, it was against the rules of their order, as well as the laws of hospitality, to allow a search of the premises, even for such a man.

Only when he was found to have disappeared had they been reluctantly convinced, and since by then he was undoubtedly well away, they had permitted a search. As expected, nothing had been found. Distressed, they had noticed the wagon coming along the road and had made arrangements with the driver to take the coffin on his load.

Keith hid a smile at the manner in which McManus had hoodwinked them. The man was a scoundrel, but once again he had proved himself a man of parts.

"I don't think there's really much mystery as to what has happened," Keith explained. "Of course McManus overheard when the Vigilantes came looking for him. Knowing that they'd probably hang him if they got their hands on him, he had to find some way of escape. What he did, obviously, was to remove the body of Brother Sebastian from the box, then take his place.

Then, when he got a chance, he climbed from the coffin and got away."

Couched in such terms, the incredible became not only possible but logical, save for one thing. What could have happened to the body of Sebastian?

Obviously, these people needed help. They made no overstatement what saying that they were other-worldly, hardly fitted to cope with such problems. The stage driver, already resigned to more delay, was willing, as were the other passengers. They accompanied the Brothers back to the mission, and again it took Keith only a minute to solve the mystery.

He surveyed the empty room, studied the floor, and found, not at all to his surprise, that the wide board lifted easily. Under it, to their mingled horror and relief, was the body.

This time the stagecoach was pressed into service, and there was more delay while the funeral was finally conducted. Then, as there was no sign of the missing driver, Keith explained that the wagon belonged to him and took charge of it.

"You'd better go on with the stage," he suggested to Martha. "It will be a lot faster, as well as more comfortable. I'll follow with the wagon as quickly as possible, and join you at Benton."

Her refusal did not surprise him. He was beginning to understand the spirit of this woman who journeyed so valiantly beside him, who had braved travel in time

f war and to an untamed land. Perhaps it was the
eligious atmosphere which inspired the terms of her
nswer, but Keith had no trouble understanding.

"Whither thou goest," she said, and though her eyes
vere suspiciously bright, her smile was assured.

18.

McManus shrugged resignedly as he punched the empty shell from the cylinder and replaced it with a fresh cartridge. It was too bad that events had finally come to this; he'd planned to keep Law alive, since there were many good reasons for doing so. He would have preferred it that way.

All at once there had been twin difficulties in the way. John Law did not look upon him with the brotherly affection which he so ardently sought to return. Being in the immediate neighborhood, he could prove a real hazard.

Equally vital, McManus needed the horse which Law rode; he had to have it. The essence of the problem was survival. That had to come ahead of all else.

Recent developments had also made Law of less importance in his planning. McManus had no doubt of his ability to execute his original scheme and to gain possession of Law's property in the East. He had intended to be meticulous about that to a point of honor, on account of Martha Law. But a new factor had been added when Martha had turned to Keith. Since she showed such disregard for him, she deserved no special consideration.

More important than all the rest was the well-stuffed money-belt which made an uncomfortable burden about his waist. Until now he had sought for wealth, and suddenly he had it. And gold, in essence, was all that counted.

"He brought it upon himself," McManus muttered. "He was in the wrong place at the wrong time. I am innocent." The simple password of the outlaws was a sheer work of genius. Enviously, he wished that he had been the one to hit upon it.

McManus gave an indifferent glance toward where Law lay near the foot of the slope. All was quiet, now that the echo of the gunshot had died. If others were around to hear, they were not close enough to be a hazard.

Circling, he came to the mouth of the coulee and spotted the thin haze of smoke. The fire had nearly burnt itself out, but the plucked sage hen, fastened on a green spit above the blaze, had a savory fragrance. McManus bit into it questioningly, finding the meat something not quite done, but edible. He carried it with him, looking about sharply.

Disappointment was strong in him as he saw the horse grazing hungrily. He had forgotten that Law would be riding the pinto. A horse so marked was a hazard.

He'd have to chance it, since he had to get away from there as fast as possible. McManus caught the horse, tightened the girth with a jerk and swung into the saddle. He cast away the partly eaten meat with a grimace of disttaste, then headed away from the road in an easterly direction. It would be safer to use a path of his own choosing from here on.

Belatedly he thought of gold in connection with Law, and hesitated. Law had been a well-to-do man in his native state, but most of that wealth had been inherited. According to rumor and speculation along the gulch, Law had achieved nothing spectacular in gaining new wealth. He had been just another of the luckless horde who passed and were forgotten. Few struck it rich, as Bill Fairweather had done.

Still, there was a chance that Law might have a money-belt, with enough in it to be worth-while. McManus shrugged and kept on going. It was too late to turn back, and the surprising part was that he really wanted no more gold—not, at least, in the form of dust or nuggets, which he had to carry. Even gold could become a burden.

The stagecoach was long out of sight, the dust of its passing only a faint haze hanging in the air. The sound of the gun had reached the driver, and while such a noise was hard to place among the hills, he had whipped up the horses, allowing them no breather on the way to the crest of the divide. There had been too much trouble and delay already; he did not intend to risk more by any display of curiosity.

The laden wagon moved more slowly, Keith allowing the horses frequent stops for rest. From their looks, the driver he had hired had used them hard since leaving Pine Grove.

Martha had been diverted by the episode at the mission. Though she sympathized with the Brothers, nonetheless some of the aspects of the situation were more comic than tragic. She could not but smile, picturing McManus in the role of a corpse. But the reflection that he might be prowling in the vicinity was less pleasant.

"At least he didn't want to be bothered with a wagon," Keith pointed out. "He had the chance to take this outfit if he'd cared to. But he's in a hurry."

"I suppose so. Shouldn't we hurry, too?"

"That's a question that can be answered both ways," Keith explained. "In one way, I'd just as soon have him a little farther ahead." Martha understood that she was the reason, and did not question him. "Also, I contracted to deliver this freight at Benton, and that is an obligation. There's a third reason, maybe the most important.

"McManus might not have been in such a hurry if

he'd guessed that we're riding above a cache of gold," Keith went on. "I made a strike last summer—not a big one, but worth having. This seemed like a good way to get it out from the gulch."

Martha gave him a quick glance, pleased that he should confide the secret to her. Before either of them could say more, the horses swerved and snorted. Keith kicked on the brake and shoved the reins into Martha's hands. Then he was over the wheel and down.

Something lay almost hidden among the old grass and brush near the road. The curled, brown leaves of buck-brush served as a cover. Like the stage, they might have passed without noticing anything had not the horse caught the alien scent of blood.

Martha's impulse was to close her eyes, not to look. Already she had seen far too much that was unpleasant on the journey. Instead, she gasped and came down and stood beside Keith.

"Is—is he—?" Her stiff lips hesitated over the word.

Keith had slid a hand inside the shirt, feeling for a heartbeat. "He's alive," he returned, but beyond that, there was little to say by way of reassurance. Law was unconscious, and he had lost considerable blood. Making a more careful examination, Keith found where the bullet had entered; the wound was no more than a bluish puncture. It had passed clear through the body, and most of the bleeding was at the point of exit.

Whether or not the lead had worked serious damage

in its passage, it was beyond Keith's ability to estimate. Apparently it had missed a vital part, but narrowly.

Grimmest of all was the certainty that Law had been shot in the back. It had been a deliberate act of bushwhack, planned as cold-blooded murder. He probably had not been aware of any danger until the shot had struck him down.

There was no doubt in the minds of either bystander as to who had fired that shot. Almost certainly it had been McManus.

They worked to stop the bleeding, to bandage the wounds as well as possible. Then Keith lifted the unconscious man in his arms and carried him to the wagon. Martha hurried ahead, snatching a blanket, spreading the buffalo robe, making a bed of sorts in the back. She cradled her brother's head in her lap as Keith eased him down.

"We'll have to keep on to Sun River," Keith decided, picking up the reins again. "That is the best chance—about the only one that I can see."

He explained his decision, discussing other aspects of the situation with her. Had Brother Sebastian been alive, with his undoubted skill and experience, it would have paid to turn back to the mission. But with life there disrupted and no one with skill in charge, such a course would gain nothing.

Only two towns lay ahead. He doubted if there would be any physician at the settlement along the

Sun, if indeed there would be one at Benton itself. But at least there would be houses, and some people with a measure of skill in caring for the sick. If Law could survive the jouncing of the wagon that far, he might stand a chance.

"How long?" Martha's lips formed the question.

"It will be a long day," Keith answered reluctantly, and urged the horses ahead, as they wanted to take another breather. At long last they were nearing the summit. On the eastern side, the long slopes ran for miles, reaching gradually to the Sun, then on to the greater tide of the Missouri. Now it would be mostly downhill, and the going would be comparatively easy, but it was a long way. Keith doubted if there were any ranches en route.

From Sun River to Benton was another long haul, since the Sun joined the Big Muddy a long way above Great Falls, which stood as an insurmountable barrier against the farther ascent of river boats. A man on horseback, careless of the animal he bestrode, could make good time. A creaking wagon was another matter.

The horses moved more readily with the wagon shoving at their heels, instead of a drag in the traces. Now the land lay open and wide. To the south reared Square Butte, a huge foundation for a mountain, although the hill itself was mysteriously missing. It made a landmark visible for long distances.

Despite the distances, there was no sign of a man on

orseback. Keith doubted if McManus would follow
e road, but it would make little difference. The ap-
earance of openness was deceiving. There were many
ills and valleys, trees, stones and natural coverts to
fford shelter much of the time.

Haze was shutting out the sun, overspreading the
ky. The breeze puffed from a draw, the unseemly
armth of the last few days suddenly lost. The weather
as due for a change, and at that season, it might mean
old and blizzard raging across the wastelands; storm,
hich could pounce with the devastating swiftness and
eadly impact of a falcon.

Keith urged the horses to a trot. The threat of storm
as one more reason for haste, one more reason they
ust catch up with McManus. Now the odds increased
ith every mile. If they managed, it would be as much
matter of luck as anything.

Luck could work either for or against either of them.
lready, the last river packet might have started back
ownstream, in which case there would be nothing
ore until the following spring. That was a risk they
ll ran.

In any case, there would probably be only one boat
eft, and it might depart at any hour. On the other
and, days or weeks could still elapse. Schedules were
ncertain, and word concerning them seldom reached
he camps. It was as much a matter of luck, of the
kill of captain and pilot, as it was of planning.

McManus might reach Fort Benton in time to board a boat and be gone ahead of them. Or luck might run in their favor. That was definitely a chance to be taken.

The matter of first and vital import was to get Law to a bed, to give him a chance to rest and such care and skill as were available.

Keith looked back, and Martha raised her head, striving to smile. The tremulous quiver of her lip twisted his heart. She was cramped and uncomfortable, but uncomplaining. Law had not stirred since they had loaded him aboard.

There was a stream ahead, a creek brawling down from the divide. Keith allowed the horses to drink. Martha got down and stretched, getting a drink. They washed Law's face, trying to get him to swallow, with little result. He was still alive, and that was to the good, but it seemed about all. The sun had vanished, crowded from the sky. Even across the open miles there was no sign of a town, no visible rise of smoke in the still air.

When finally they approached it, the town was asleep, the buildings dark huddles. The river swirled like ink between woody banks. By then, the horses were barely plodding, while riding had become an agony of cramped flesh.

By the time they found shelter, half the town had been aroused. There was no hotel, but a family took Law in, making room for Martha also. Keith stretched out in the hay at the livery barn. As he had feared, there was no doctor.

The morning was gray, heavily overcast. Storm was definitely on the way. But Law seemed better, sleeping rather than in a coma, now he had a chance to rest. Keith had another piece of luck, finding a man willing to drive the wagon on to Benton. Martha would remain with her brother. Keith obtained a horse and went on. There had to be a reckoning.

19.

The bullet came out of nowhere, as furious as a mad-
dened wasp—a wasp belatedly abroad, apprehensive of
winter and death, driving toward some shelter which
was as elusive as a phantom. McManus heard the whine
of the lead, and his pinto cayuse snorted and jerked its
head as though stung by the sound. The crash of the
gun rolled like a belated thunder.

Whether the shot had been aimed with intent to kill
or sent close as a warning, other bullets would follow,
and there could be no doubt as to how they would be
aimed. The pony had already made a choice, lengthening its stride in frantic leaps. McManus encouraged it
to greater efforts, heading for the doubtful sanctuary
of broken lands.

As a covert, these hills left much to be desired.
They had taken on a quality of smoothness, of long
easy slopes pleasantly grassed. Here and there were
shallow depressions, strange-looking hollows; these
were buffalo wallows, too shallow to be of any use

as a cover, indicative of the excellent range. They were further proof that it was good country for hunting, whether the quarry was four-legged or two.

High and broken hills lay only a few miles along his back trail, wherein he might have lost himself like a shadow at the sun's declining; but he could not go back, and his first guess was correct. He was hunted, a man wanted, dead or alive. If they had a choice, they would take him dead.

McManus soon made sure that a quartette were after him. It was reasonable to suppose that these would be the men whom he had eluded back at the Mission, which to them would be a rankling memory. They had kept riding widely, and now their persistence was paying off.

Whether they were after him or after the rider of the pinto pony was another moot question. The possible difference in identity was unlikely to make much difference. Being mounted on a pinto had betrayed him, and his refusal to halt and give an account of himself confirmed their suspicions.

Though he had known worse, odds of four to one were not to his liking. The range at the moment was a little long, but while he was glimpsed, guns made a chorus as eager as hunting hounds. They subsided as the sobbing horse ducked out of sight, and McManus assessed his chances. Night was too far away to come to his rescue. If anything was to be done, he had to do it himself, which meant whittling down the odds.

There, too, he was handicapped. All four had demonstrated that they carried rifles, while he had only a six-gun. Bumps showed in the distance, a scattered cluster of boulders, a shelter of sorts if he could reach them. It could prove a trap, with them coming at him from all four sides, but it would be better than nothing. The problem was to live long enough to reach the stones.

In a straight run the rifles would decide it. He had to circle, making use of such broken country as was available. But at least he had nothing to lose by trying.

They were wasting a lot of lead, over-eager to shoot, scarcely aiming. McManus pulled up and waited, and picked his own target as they came into sight, surprised at finding him so close. He toppled one man cleanly from the saddle, confusing the others. Even so, it had been a near thing. There were holes in his hat and tears in his coat sleeve where bullets had plucked.

The boulders were just ahead, but the pinto was wheezing, lungs like a bellows, lathered with sweat despite the increasing chill in the air. McManus debated his course. He was no lightweight to begin with, and the money-belt made a heavy difference in the load which the horse carried. The extra weight might spell the difference between escape and the sudden termination of the chase.

Should he lighten the load by discarding the money-belt, the choice might save his life. McManus rejected the notion. To part with gold was unthinkable.

He dismounted and took shelter between a pair of the boulders; now they would be unsure of his position. One man made a target, and McManus shot, then shook his head in disbelief. He'd scored a hit, but not as he'd intended. Instead of the man, the pony had collapsed. Its rider jumped clear and dodged for cover, but by then the other riders were spreading out, starting to circle. Knowing his position, they hoped to get McManus between a crossfire.

It was time to gamble, and he rode ahead again, passing close to one of the pair, where discovery might have been fatal. Not expecting such a move, the other horseman was looking the other way. The ruse gained vital time.

McManus kept on, to put as much distance between himself and the hunters as he could. It added up to a mile, and would have been more had he dared push his weary horse. It was faltering even at a trot, and his only reassurance was that the others were tiring also.

The remaining pair must have been having second thoughts about the value of the chase, or the danger of being killed themselves instead of him. The slopes were still long and easy, but there was enough distance between them so that he could keep out of sight much of the time.

The day was wearing away, turned gray and old. The two riders were strung out, following doggedly, but one was half a mile behind the other, and neither was able to make a race of it.

Having left the road behind as soon as he had gotten the pinto, McManus had not come within sight of it again. He headed in the general direction he wished to go, east by a little south. The haze had eaten up the sky, and now it was taking gulps of the long slope of the plain, so that on all sides the horizons seemed to shrink and draw in on themselves.

McManus allowed his thoughts to run ahead. It would be pleasant to get aboard a river packet, to lodge snugly in a room of his own. With each turn of the paddle-wheel, they'd be following the sun south—

His horse stumbled, and the reverie was broken. Neither spur nor quirt had any effect. The pinto had been ridden to the limit of endurance, and nothing short of food and rest could revive it. A second time it stumbled, going to its knees. Not until he swung reluctantly to the ground did it come slowly erect again, swaying like a drunken creature.

McManus broke into a wild tirade, then caught himself and put a tight rein on his anger. Rage would not help. It was too late now to lighten the burden by casting aside his money-belt. The two riders clung like nemesis to his trail.

He took a few steps, tugging the reluctant pony

along by the reins, fighting a sudden rush of panic. The pony was finished, done. So, too, would he be. The hunters would close in from opposite directions. The superior range of their rifles would decide the matter without risk on their part. Darkness was still too far away to help.

He let go of the reins, and the pony's head drooped, its heavy breath puffing a tiny cloud of dust among the cured grasses. He might shoot it, then take shelter behind it, but prudence dictated against that. He was momentarily out of sight of the others, and even a few minutes of unrestricted movement might bring some new possibility. His luck could not desert him now.

Walking, he was soon out of sight of the pony. But in another couple of minutes the hunters would sight it and understand—

McManus blinked, awed in spite of himself. Apparently the devil did look after his own. Or would the Old Scratch be concerned with this? The implications of the situation should bring a tail-twisting chuckle from him. McManus raised his voice in a hail.

For all its unexpectedness, the situation was not too hard to understand. Brother Jonas and Brother Felix had been dispatched from the Mission, to go to Sun River after supplies. They had not returned as expected, and the delay was not hard to figure out.

At the Mission, Brother Sebastian had been the

guiding light, the man of experience, the motivating force. As long as he told them what to do and showed them how, the Brothers did reasonably well. Without Sebastian they were the veriest tenderfeet, well-intentioned but almost helpless.

McManus had stayed long enough to be sure of that. This pair clearly followed the pattern. Somewhere on the way home they had taken a wrong turn, leaving the wheel-trace behind, and had begun wandering lost and helpless on the trackless sweep of plain. Apparently they had been wandering ever since.

The wagon was within a stone's-throw of McManus, the slow-moving team pointed in the wrong direction. A man on a horse rode near it, clearly sharing the driver's bewilderment as to where they should go.

The thrusting ridge of hills to the west, the glimpse of the winding River of the Sun visible to the north, should have been landmarks enough for most men, but to these hapless pilgrims they apparently were without meaning. If they had depended on the sun as a compass, now there was no sun.

That served well enough to explain what had happened and their presence there, far from the road. McManus had scant interest in any of it, save as he was affected. Here was a reasonably fresh horse, and he had to have a horse.

Brother Felix was a tall, lank man, no more at ease in the saddle than in a wilderness. He looked around at the call, staring doubtfully, then hopefully, and kicked his horse to a clumsy trot, tugging it about. His face wore a look of wistful uncertainty.

McManus added to his astonishment with his greeting.

"You are Brother Felix, from the Mission?"

Felix blinked, then bobbed an acknowledgment.

"I am Felix," he granted. "But you have the advantage of me."

"No, it is the other way around," McManus denied. "You are mounted, while I am afoot." He groaned, and there was no trouble making it convincing. "I fear I can walk no farther."

Felix was instantly sympathetic. He glanced toward the wagon, which had halted, hesitated, then made up his mind, dismounting in a wild flurry of robes.

"Then mount my animal," he urged. "He is a gentle beast—for the most part—and you can ride him, at least as far as the wagon."

"You are very kind." McManus pulled himself into the saddle with surprising celerity. He pointed toward the dimming mass of the square butte, showing well to the south. Despite the haze, it was still visible.

"That butte lies to the south," he explained. "Your Mission lies to the west, on the far side of the hills." Again he swept an arm in a gesture. "Ride toward the hills, heading south again until you reach the road; then follow it. There will be room for you to ride on the wagon."

Felix looked puzzled.

"But you—are you not going with us?"

"I have business in the other direction," McManus returned curtly. "One favor for another. Your horse for setting you straight."

He started to swing it, but paused as Felix raised his voice in anguished protest.

"But you—surely you would not steal our horse?"

"I need it, and it was doing you no good," McManus replied. He restrained himself, then surprised himself with a sudden impulse. The dollar-sized nugget which he had offered Stennis gleamed dully in his hand.

"This will pay for the horse, and something besides for the work of your mission," he growled, and tossed the gold at the bewildered Felix. He raked the horse with his spurs, then was gone, not looking back.

20.

The remaining three score miles on the road to Benton would be as grim as any Keith had ever ridden. The cold was increasing. They had found shelter and hospitality at Sun River, and Law was being cared for as well as could be managed. When or if he regained consciousness, he would find Martha beside him, to help and encourage him. A man could ask no better.

Somewhere ahead rode McManus. That, at least, was the name by which he was infamous in the territory. Keith was aware that he had, at one time or another, used the names of a dozen different people, just as he took whatever he fancied.

Sooner or later, Keith was confident of catching up with the man. The knowledge that he'd face a showdown with a killer did not particularly worry him, though the prospect was as bleak as the weather. And for the time of year, the weather could hardly have been worse.

Snow had commenced during the forenoon, the storm gradually thickening. The flinty flakes were caught and wracked by a moaning wind which tormented the prairie. The day was uncomfortably cold and getting worse, but he had to keep going.

McManus was as near to repentance that day as he ever came, repentant of the deal he had made. The shaggy brown cayuse which Brother Felix had ridden had the look of a good animal, with a build for speed and stamina. Perhaps it possessed both, but if so, it was intent on keeping those qualities a secret. Accustomed to a pampered existence, to picking its own path and gait, it responded grudgingly to the spurs, and somehow managed to loiter even when pretending to be at a full run.

McManus was in a savage mood by the time they reached the Sun, running as steel-gray as the weather and looking like anything but what its name implied. Far from the road as he was, there was no bridge, and though it was low water season, the river thereabouts had an unpromising aspect. Yet cross he must, and without delay. Night was coming down, and he had to be on the far side when he camped.

It turned out that he was, though not in the way he'd intended. Halfway across, showering the water with clumsy hoof strokes, the brown cayuse slipped and flopped into an unexpected hole, going immediately out of sight and taking McManus down with him.

If this was a form of baptism, he had no liking for it. When they finally reached the far shore, the horse shook itself indifferently and seemed no worse for the wetting. But McManus was soaked, and the wind had an icy thrust.

There was only one thing to do, if he was to survive the night, and it taxed his strength to the utmost to accomplish that. He carried matches, wrapped to remain waterproof. There was dry wood handy where flood waters had piled drift high along the bank, leaving it to bleach through the long suns of summer. Yet to get a fire going, with ice congealing in his clothes, was a bitter chore.

A fire there, in fairly open country, with a big enough blaze to warm and dry himself, was a hazard. Such a beacon might be seen for a long way on a dark night. Still, he had no choice but to risk it.

It was midnight before he was dry, and by then the supply of fuel was running low. When he went on the next day, his mood was increasingly savage. He'd missed a succession of meals, and was stiff and lame from cold and exertion. He had a feeling that time was running out. Worse, Keith might be—and probably was—close on his heels. For others he had mostly contempt, but Keith was a menace.

He took to looking back uneasily. There was nothing to see in the thickening storm, though his uneasiness was justified. Only the snow kept him hidden

from Keith, now no more than a mile behind. Mc-
Manus followed the road, aware that without it he
would soon be lost.

By the time early darkness closed down, the land
was white, and the storm showed no signs of diminishing. No lights were visible until the town was immediately at hand, and even then they were uncertain
gleams, as though a misplaced star had been caught
and almost smothered in the snow.

McManus found one livery stable, Keith another.
That was chance, as was their choice a few minutes
later of restaurants on opposite sides of the street.
Each man heard the same piece of news as he ate. The
Memphis Belle was in port, having arrived that forenoon. Undoubtedly, she was the last packet which
would make the run that year. Because of the threat-
ening weather, the possibility of hampering ice if he
delayed too long, her captain planned to cast off the
lines and drop down-river with the first light of dawn.

Both men considered the news and reached similar
conclusions. Then they returned to the stables, making their beds in the hay. Each was at the verge of
exhaustion, and with his hunger satisfied, sleep had to
come before anything else. There would be time enough
for other matters in the new day.

McManus was elated. Despite the setbacks along the
way, his luck was holding. Perhaps it had been because
of his gesture in tossing the nugget to the black-robe.

any case, he wouldn't miss the gold. Entirely aside from what might develop in the East, and with war here were always uncertainties, still he was by way of being rich.

If his original plan carried through—and now that he could apply the proper greasing to certain itchy palms, was more likely to than before—he'd be in the position he'd long dreamed of. He could settle down with a fine estate and play the role of country squire, benevolent gentleman divorced from his past.

Even if some details did not fully work out, he still would have nothing to complain of.

It was true that he'd failed where Martha Law was concerned, but she had been mostly a means to an end. He asked only one more gift of fate now—the chance to settle scores with Keith before departing that wild land. If he could not have her, neither should Keith.

Events could not have been better timed for his purpose, even had he known the sailing date in advance. This way, he'd contrive to go aboard the *Belle* at the last moment. That would cut risk to a minimum, and once he was on board and in midstream, the worries would be the captain's and the pilot's, not his. Nothing could stop him then.

There was a good chance that the boat would be full, perhaps overloaded, but that was no cause for worry. He had the wherewithal to pay for what he wanted, and when a man could pay, he could generally get what he asked for.

The hoarse whistle of the river boat awakened Keith, as he had counted on it doing. It mounted to a ghostly wail, hanging, quivering, and died in a sob. It was still dark outside, and quite cold, even inside the barn. A look around as he opened the door assured him that the storm continued, increasing rather than diminishing in intensity. The warning whistle was to let those who might be interested know that the *Memphis Belle* was preparing to get under way.

There would be a second blast of the whistle before the lines were cast off some time later. He could picture the feverish last-minute activity, as smoke belched and was whipped away in the wind, and men labored to load the last of the freight or get aboard themselves. There was always a hurlyburly before such a sailing; things had a slightly unreal air to landlubbers such as himself. The driving storm would make it worse.

Keith had little doubt but that McManus would be preparing to embark. The outlaw had a way of accomplishing what he set out to do, and it was reasonable that he would be on hand. Even so, there was no undue cause for haste. McManus was too crafty to risk showing himself at the boat until the last possible moment.

Breakfast would have to wait. In any case, Keith was not hungry. The imminence of a showdown had taken away his appetite.

The job had to be done, and it had been assigned to

im. There could be no dodging, no turning back short
f whatever might result. He was resigned to that, but
was not a prospect to look forward to. Even an assur-
nce of success would scarcely sweeten the task, for if
e won, McManus had to lose.

McManus deserved the fate he had meted out to
thers. Yet, cold-blooded and calculating as he was,
IcManus was a man, impelled by the same emotions
s other men, knowing fear and hunger as well as
varice and triumph. If not a worthy opponent, he was
ertainly formidable, and Keith had come to feel
espect, almost a grudging admiration for the effici-
ncy with which he operated. Win, lose or draw, the
10wdown would be as coldly bitter as the weather.

Keith moved out into the storm. To reach his desti-
ation it was necessary to depend on memory more
1an on sight, for the snow and dawn blanketed town
nd country. Fort Benton sprawled above the northern
ank of the Missouri, with low bluffs crowding the
ver. It was an army fort, as its name implied, but it
ad become a trading center for Indians and trappers,
nd since the discovery of gold at Bannack and Alder
ulch, it had become an important port. It marked
1e end of travel by water, the beginning of a busy
ver'.and supply route.

None of that could be more than guessed in the
loom of the winter morning, despite the stir caused
y the warning whistle and the imminence of the de-

parture of the last boat. Lights were lost as completely as they had been the evening before; the snow-clogged streets all but deserted. Someone shouted, the sound echoing lost and lonely in the slow gray dawn, and that was all.

Keith turned toward the river, moving partly by memory, partly by instinct. There was nothing visible to indicate where it might be.

He left the straggling line of buildings behind, buffeted by the full fury of the storm. Bad as it had been the day before, now it had become a blizzard. A man might fall and perish in the middle of the town, unsuspected, unmissed by others only a few feet away.

Keith sensed rather than saw the ghostly figure, barely recognizing McManus in the heavily clothed, bear-like figure crowding suddenly at him. Luck had once again been with the outlaw, for McManus had seen him first.

It was cold, and there was a certain amount of risk with a gun, which would shout an alarm. But the darkness and snow were in his favor, and this was showdown, the sort of final settlement he'd waited for. McManus was not surprised to find Keith there, for he had expected something of the sort. His luck was still holding. The comfortable feel of the laden money belt was evidence of how good it was.

Keith saw the gun jump out from the coat and tried

desperately to twist aside as it thundered in his face. He went down, his foot catching on a hidden obstruction, and felt the burn of powder across his cheek. It took a moment of floundering before he could regain his feet and plunge after McManus, loosening his own gun in holster.

McManus was ahead, confident that the shot at point-blank range had achieved its purpose. He could make out the lights of the *Memphis Belle,* showing dimly in the growing light. Her hoarse whistle, made more strident by the cold, slashed mournfully at the buffeting elements, warning of her imminent departure.

McManus quickened his pace. He had timed matters perfectly. As far as Keith was concerned, he felt no compunction; only satisfaction. He broke into a clumsy run, seeing the gangplank being drawn back. He opened his mouth to shout, but the last-minute flurry of noise drowned it.

Then he heard another shout, and turned his head incredulously. Keith was coming along behind him, narrowing the distance between them.

McManus' stride faltered, then quickened. There was no time to turn to settle accounts; he could not afford to miss the boat. Besides, the gunfire would attract unwanted attention, and there might be others besides Keith who would take an interest in him.

A narrow stretch of black water loomed between and shore and the boat, but not enough to be concerned about. McManus freed his arms from the heavy overcoat and flung it to the side, so that he would be unencumbered by its clumsiness. Once on board, headed for a warmer clime, he'd have no need for it.

Keith raised his gun, aiming carefully, then paused.

McManus launched himself, dimly aware of shadowy figures all about, but disregarding them. Another instant and nothing could stop him.

A choking gasp sent his breath out in a steaming cloud, as he felt astonishment and dismay. There was time for no more. The distance was no greater than he'd estimated, no more than he'd leaped many times before. But it was as though the spring had gone from his legs, now his pockets were laden with lead. Even the discarded heavy coat made no appreciable difference.

Too late he realized that the weight of the stuffed money-belt was enough to make the difference. His outstretched fingers scraped the edge of the boat and slid away. Then the dark waters which swirled alongside the packet closed over him, and the weight dragged him down as relentlessly as doom.

Like the others who had seen the jump, Keith waited, but no ripple broke the surface. Keith returned the revolver to his holster. One man exclaimed, with awe and disbelief:

"Looks like he went down like a stone. Kind of surprisin', that it happened that way."

Keith might have explained, but he did not. After the *Belle* churned out into the river and was lost to sight, he plodded back up the street, still with scant appetite for breakfast. As soon as the storm ended, he'd head back for Sun River.

The sun was shining as he approached, a streak of silver along the river. He was tying his horse when Martha saw him and burst from the house, and the next instant she was in his arms.

"Harley! I've been afraid—"

She was torn between laughter and tears. But Law was awake and strong enough to smile when she led Keith back to the room, and nothing else mattered. There had been treasure for the finding along the road, and Keith and McManus alike had been lucky, according to each man's way of looking at it. The Sun today was a river of promise.